THE BAKER STREET MURDERS

An Augusta Peel Mystery Book 7

EMILY ORGAN

The Augusta Peel Series

Death in Soho
Murder in the Air
The Bloomsbury Murder
The Tower Bridge Murder
Death in Westminster
Murder on the Thames
The Baker Street Murders
Death in Kensington

Chapter 1

JULY 1911.

A train was waiting in the station, hissing with steam. She ran across the footbridge as fast as she could, desperate to catch it.

The engine gave a whistle as she reached the platform. She darted for the nearest carriage, pulled open the door, and leapt inside. Then she pulled the door shut with a resounding slam.

'Good grief!' said a lady sitting in the compartment. 'You almost frightened me to death with that noise!' She wore a large hat decorated with artificial flowers.

'Sorry.' She slumped into the seat opposite and recovered her breath.

The train pulled out of the station and the lady in the hat peered at her. 'Are you alright?'

'I'm fine.' She pulled a handkerchief from her handbag and wiped her tear-stained face.

'You don't look alright.'

'I just got a little hot while running to catch the train.'

There were no further questions from the lady in the hat. Instead, she pulled some knitting from her bag and set to work on it.

The regular clack of knitting needles and the rattle of the carriage combined into a comforting sound. She rested her head back and closed her eyes.

But scenes she wanted to forget came back to her. They flashed in her mind like moving pictures in a cinema.

Opening her eyes again, she caught the lady in the hat giving her a curious look. She glanced away and opened her handbag. Shoved into the inner pocket was the bundle of ten-shilling notes. She had never seen so much money before. It had to be more than she earned in a year.

But she didn't want the money. It didn't make her feel better about anything. It only served to remind her what had happened.

She closed her bag and looked out at north London passing by the window.

If only she hadn't listened to Alexander Miller.

Chapter 2

TEN YEARS LATER.

'A box of books from a mysterious donor!' said Fred when Augusta arrived at her second-hand bookshop on a warm June morning.

She placed Sparky's canary cage on the counter and peered into the box of books which sat on the floor. 'This was left outside the shop?' she asked. People had left books on the shop's doorstep before, but never this many.

'Yes. It was sitting outside the door when I arrived this morning,' said Fred. He lifted out some of the books. 'We've got *Howard's End* here, *The Wind in the Willows*, *Piccadilly Jim*. That's a very funny book.' He handed the books to Augusta and looked through the rest. '*Night and Day*,' he said, '*The Phoenix and the Carpet*, *The Scarlet Pimpernel*, *The Enchanted Castle*, *Kim*, *The Grand Babylon Hotel*, and *The Invisible Man*. And that's not all of them.'

'It's nice to have some more children's books,' said Augusta. 'And the others are all popular titles.' She laid the books out on the counter 'These have been well looked after. With a bit of luck, they won't require too much repair. Just a clean and I'll need to check they have all their pages. I wonder who left the box here?'

'I wonder too,' said Fred. 'If they had brought the box in while we were open, we could have offered them some money for the books. Shall I put them back in the box and carry it into the workshop for you?'

'Thank you, Fred. They can be added to my growing repair pile. I'll put the kettle on.'

Later that day, Augusta looked through the books in her workshop. She decided to deal with the ones which were in good condition first. They wouldn't require too much work on them before they could be sold in her shop.

Night and Day by Virginia Woolf was almost as good as new. Augusta checked it had all of its pages and cleaned the cover with a damp cloth and a little soap. *The Grand Babylon Hotel* by Arnold Bennett was also easily cleaned. Then the *Invisible Man* by H.G. Wells caught Augusta's eye. It had a scarlet cover, and she smiled at the picture on it which showed a headless and limbless figure seated in a chair and wearing a long smoking jacket.

Augusta opened the book and began checking the pages were present and intact. She was about a quarter of the way through when she realised something was tucked between the pages.

She pulled it out. It was a small envelope addressed in untidy handwriting to a lady in Notting Hill. The postmark was dated July 1911 and the envelope had been neatly cut open. Augusta put the book down and pulled the letter out of the envelope. It was written on thin paper and folded twice. She unfolded the paper to reveal more of the untidy handwriting. In the top right corner was written: "18th July 1911, 72 Baker Street."

Had the letter been hidden in the book for ten years? Augusta sat down on a stool and began to decipher the handwriting. Before long, she could read the complete letter.

My Dearest Louisa,

I apologise a fortnight has passed since my last letter, but my time has been taken up by a recent, troubling incident which I shall now describe to you.

I have mentioned my friend, Alexander Miller, to you before. Like me, he works as a clerk in the accounts department of the Great Western Railway. By coincidence, he also lives in Baker Street. In a flat at number 15. I have told you about our shared enjoyment of cycling and the many day excursions we have taken at weekends. This summer we have cycled as far as Windsor, Epsom and the Chiltern Hills. As you know, I have always enjoyed cycling, and it's been extremely enjoyable having a friend to share my adventures with. We have stopped for picnics in glorious locations and visited some very charming churches and public houses along the way, too.

Just over a fortnight ago, on Sunday 3rd July, we were due to meet for a cycle to Richmond Park. Our usual arrangement was to meet at nine o'clock on a Sunday morning in Portman Square. I arrived on time for our rendezvous, but Alexander didn't appear. Tardiness is not in his character, so I called at his flat. There was no answer, which was most unusual. I decided he must have been detained somewhere as part of an emergency and went for a short bicycle ride on my own.

I called at his address again and received no response. I spoke to neighbours and couldn't find anyone who had seen him during the weekend.

Perplexed, I went to work as usual on the Monday morning and was saddened when my friend didn't make an appearance. I told the accounts officer of my concerns and he called at Alexander's address that evening. There was no response.

As the week progressed, there was still no sign of him. The accounts officer sent him a letter, and I continued to ask neighbours if they had seen anything of him. I wondered if some family business has taken him away. I know he has a sister in Camden Town, but she's married and I don't know her surname to find her.

Although I can understand that urgent business makes demands on a man, I can't understand why Alexander hasn't communicated with anyone. He's in danger of losing his job. The accounts officer says we can't hold out for him much longer and another clerk may need to be recruited to fill his position.

I wondered if Alexander had fallen dangerously ill and been unable to summon help for himself. In desperation yesterday, I made a report to the local police station. After hearing my concerns, a constable agreed to break into Alexander's flat. Although I was relieved not to find Alexander there seriously unwell (or worse), I was also bitterly disappointed that there was no sign of him. The flat was neat and tidy, as if Alexander had merely just walked out of it. His bicycle was propped against the wall in the hallway.

I don't suppose there's much more anyone can do about it now. Perhaps Alexander's family is concerned about him too. I am watching the building which houses his flat like a hawk, hoping I shall catch sight of them or other friends who are concerned about him.

I'm sorry to trouble you with this strange tale, Louisa. I hope that when I see you next, I will have joyful news regarding Alexander Miller.

Soon it will be the one-year anniversary of your marriage. I shall endeavour to put myself in a happier mood before I call on you and Simon to celebrate the happy occasion!

Your loving brother,
John

Chapter 3

Augusta went into the shop and read the letter to Fred.

'What an intriguing story,' he said when she had finished. 'I wonder if Alexander was ever found?'

'I wonder that too.'

'And the date on the letter is 1911? Ten years ago. The mystery must have been solved by now.'

'I hope so. And I hope it was good news. I don't know what the letter was doing in the book. Maybe it was used as a bookmark.'

'That's the most likely explanation. And the woman it's addressed to is presumably the person who left the box of books on the doorstep.'

'It could be the same person, couldn't it? Her name is Louisa.' Augusta looked at the envelope again. 'Her surname is Bradshaw, and she lives at 35 Oxford Gardens in Notting Hill. Or she did when her brother John wrote to her. She could have changed address since then.'

'We could check the directory to see if Mr and Mrs Bradshaw are still listed at the same place. I pass Holborn

Library on my walk home, I can check the directory in there if you like.'

'Thank you, Fred, that would be helpful. And if Louisa Bradshaw is still there, I can call on her and offer her payment for the books. I can also ask her what happened to Alexander Miller.'

'I'm trying to think of reasons why he could have gone missing,' said Fred. 'Perhaps he witnessed a terrible crime and had to be protected from the people who committed it. His life could have been in danger, so he had to leave everything and move elsewhere without telling anyone.'

'That's an interesting idea, Fred. It sounds like a good story for a novel too. I'd like to read that book.'

'Or perhaps he had a forbidden love and the pair of them eloped without a word to anyone.'

'Goodness, that could be possible, couldn't it?'

'Or he had an accident, hit his head and lost his memory. Then he lay in a hospital somewhere where no one knew anything about him.'

'His family would have found him in the end.'

'Perhaps that's what happened. Or he never recovered from the accident and had to be put in an institution.'

'You have a lot of ideas about this, Fred.'

'I'm worried he had an accident now. And maybe it was near water. If he fell into a river, a canal, or a lake in one of the parks, then he may have never resurfaced.'

'That's a sad thought. I really hope it didn't happen. I like to think he turned up again safe and well.'

'I hope so too.'

'With a bit of luck, we can find Louisa Bradshaw and she can tell us.'

Chapter 4

'THE MYSTERIOUS CASE OF ALEXANDER MILLER,' said
Philip once Augusta had read the letter to him.

He and Augusta sat in a pair of easy chairs which he
had recently purchased for his new office. The room was a
little less spartan now. There was a rug on the floor and a
couple of prints on the walls which showed London scenes.
Since setting himself up as a private detective, Philip had
worked on a handful of cases and his office now felt like a
proper workplace. He had even earned enough to have his
own telephone installed.

'I'm planning to ask Mrs Bradshaw what became of
Alexander Miller,' said Augusta.

'I might have guessed you already had plans to look
into it,' said Philip with a smile.

'I'm going to offer her some money for the box of
books she donated, too. Many of them are in excellent
condition. Fred is going to find out for me if she's still
living at the same address.'

The bookshelf on Philip's wall caught her eye. It still
only had one volume on it: *The Adventures of Sherlock Holmes*.

'Did you notice the interesting address Mrs Bradshaw's brother lives at?' she said.

'Baker Street.'

'Just like your favourite detective.' She nodded at the book on the shelf.

'Yes indeed. Perhaps Mrs Bradshaw's brother called on Holmes's services? He would have had the case solved in an instant.'

'I'm sure he would have.' Augusta took in a breath. There was something else she wanted to discuss with Philip, but she had delayed it because she knew the topic would anger him. 'There's another letter I need to show you,' she said.

'Not another mystery to puzzle over?'

'No.' She passed him the letter to read for himself. It was short and more legible than the previous one.

She watched a frown deepen on his face as he read it.

'This is from that worm, Ferguson!' he said.

Walter Ferguson was a news reporter at the *London Weekly Chronicle* who Augusta had encountered on a previous case. He had objected to her questioning him about his murdered colleague and had published some articles about her in revenge. He seemed keen to reveal her past and had published information about her work for British intelligence during the war.

Augusta had hoped that once her work on the case had finished, she wouldn't come across the reporter again. She wanted to forget about him. But it seemed Walter Ferguson did not want to forget about her.

Philip repeated the last line of the letter. '"I have uncovered something interesting. There never was a Mr Peel, was there? And Augusta is not your real name." What does he mean by this Augusta?'

'He means to make trouble for me.'

Augusta and Philip had taken different names when they had worked for British intelligence. Their colleagues had too. Augusta had given herself a married title. She had been in her thirties at the time and felt the title afforded her a bit more respect.

'You never reverted back to your real name after the war, did you Augusta?' said Philip. 'Unlike me. I never thought George Whitaker suited me very well. I don't know why I chose it.'

Augusta smiled. 'I thought you looked like a George.'

'Did you?'

'But you're more of a Philip.'

'Good. Because that's my real name. As for your real name, Augusta, I've never known it.'

She shrugged. 'I liked Augusta Peel too much.' Few people enquired about her fictional husband. Many seemed to assume he had died during the war.

'So how has that rat Ferguson found out your real name?' said Philip.

'He must have spoken to someone at the War Office. My real name will be in my file.'

'But that's a secret file! It's confidential. No one should be looking at our files there. And they certainly shouldn't be passing information on to news reporters! Can you remember who recruited you, Augusta?'

'Mr Wetherell.'

'Thin chap with large spectacles?'

Augusta nodded.

'He recruited me, too. He would have known your real name, but I can't imagine a chap as decent as Wetherell handing information over to that dreadful reporter. I only met him the once though.'

'Me too. In a cafe on Tottenham Court Road. I never saw him again after that.'

'I met him in a pub on Cheapside and never saw him after that, either. I wonder what became of him? And Wetherell wouldn't have been his real name. Anyway, I think Ferguson has persuaded someone to look at the files in the War Office. He could have paid them to do it.'

'They'll be in a lot of trouble if we can find out who it was.'

'Yes, they will! It could be someone relatively new who wasn't involved with our intelligence work at the time. Clearly they have no sense of loyalty. Or decency! I shall speak to the War Office about it.' Philip looked at the letter again. 'Ferguson says here that he has no plans to write more articles about you for the time being. *For the time being.* That suggests it could happen again in the future. If he publishes your real name, then it would be a serious breach of confidentiality!'

Augusta felt her stomach turn. The consequences of her true name being published were too much to bear.

'He has to be stopped, Philip,' she said. 'He can't be allowed to do this.'

Chapter 5

THE FOLLOWING DAY, Fred told Augusta that the Post Office Directory showed Mr and Mrs Bradshaw still living at 35 Oxford Gardens in Notting Hill. That afternoon, Augusta travelled by tube to Notting Hill Station and walked the short distance to the address. It was at the east end of the road in a smart row of tall Victorian terraces. Although the houses here were smaller than the houses at the western end, they were still spacious and towered four storeys high.

A housekeeper answered the door and showed her into a plush sitting room where Louisa Bradshaw joined her a few minutes later. She was about thirty and round-faced with freckles across her nose and fair bobbed hair. Her eyes were bright and intelligent and she wore a simple yet fashionable sage green day dress.

Augusta Peel introduced herself as they sat. 'I'd like to thank you for the books,' she said.

'Books?' Mrs Bradshaw pulled a puzzled expression.

'Yes. The box of books which you left outside my bookshop yesterday.'

She gave a tense, polite smile. 'There must have been a

mistake, I'm afraid. I haven't left a box of books anywhere.'

'Oh. I'm sorry to trouble you, then.' Augusta reached into her bag. 'I assumed you'd donated the books because I found this letter.' She handed it to her.

Mrs Bradshaw gasped as she looked at the envelope. 'Goodness! Where did you find this?'

'It was in one of the books in the box. That was why I'd assumed the books had belonged to you.'

'Which book was it in?'

'*The Invisible Man* by H. G. Wells.'

Mrs Bradshaw stared into the middle distance as she thought. 'Yes, that would be about right... I remember reading that book. I lent it to a friend. Some years ago now.'

'So it could have been your friend who donated the books?'

'Yes, it could have been.' Her eyes returned to the letter in her hand. 'And this was in the book! It's from John, my brother. I suppose it must have been in the book for all that time! I must have put it in there for safekeeping.'

'I hope you don't mind, but I read the letter.'

'Why should I mind?'

'Because it was a private letter written to you.'

'It was ten years ago. John used to send me a lot of letters. He enjoyed writing them. I kept them all so it's lovely to have this returned to me. Thank you, Mrs Peel.'

'Does he no longer send you letters?' asked Augusta.

She gave a sad smile. 'No. He died.'

'Oh, I'm so sorry to hear it.'

'It was ten years ago.' She looked at the postmark on the envelope. 'About five months after this letter was written, actually.'

'You must miss him a lot.'

14

'I do. He died in an accident. He fell beneath a train at Baker Street Station. It was very busy on the platform at the time and he somehow lost his footing.'

'How awful!'

Mrs Bradshaw pulled the letter out of the envelope.

'Your brother's letter is quite intriguing,' said Augusta. 'He describes the disappearance of a friend. Alexander Miller.'

'Oh, I remember now! That was very strange.'

Augusta wanted to ask her more but sat quietly as Mrs Bradshaw read the letter. 'I'd forgotten how untidy his handwriting was!' she said as her eyes scanned over the words.

When she had finished reading, Mrs Bradshaw pressed a fingertip into the corner of each eye. 'This has reminded me how much I miss him,' she said. 'How can ten years have passed already? It really doesn't seem that long ago.'

'Do you know what became of Alexander Miller?' asked Augusta.

'No. I know he wasn't found before John died. Perhaps he's been found since, I wouldn't know. But it was sad John died without ever knowing what had happened to him. They'd been good friends.'

'Did you ever meet Mr Miller?'

'No, I didn't. He was just someone who John mentioned in his letters. He was quite chatty, as you can probably tell! He wrote to me once or twice a month, even though he didn't live very far away.'

'Did he discuss his missing friend with you?'

'Oh yes. He was very worried about Alexander. And confused too. He couldn't understand how someone could completely vanish like that. He'd been to the police about it, but they hadn't been much help.'

'They didn't do anything?'

'I believe they looked for him but couldn't find him anywhere. And in a large, busy city like London, it's not surprising, is it? I can only imagine they did what they could.'

'And when your brother talked to you about Alexander Miller, did he have any clue about why he had disappeared?'

'No. None at all. It completely puzzled him. I can only hope Alexander Miller was alright in the end and is alive and well somewhere today. It was ten years ago, so who knows what happened?'

Chapter 6

FROM NOTTING HILL, Augusta travelled by tube to Baker Street. As she left the train, she thought about Mrs Bradshaw's brother, John, and the tragic accident which had claimed his life here. Baker Street station was a busy place served by four tube lines. It wasn't difficult to imagine the platforms getting so crowded that someone could slip off onto the railway tracks.

Augusta made her way to the closest police station. She reasoned it was the one which John would have visited to discuss Alexander Miller's disappearance with the police. With a bit of luck, the station still had a record of his visit.

Crawford Place police station was a Victorian red brick building with tall windows. It occupied the corner of Crawford Place and Molyneux Street. After a discussion with the desk sergeant, Augusta was introduced to Inspector Whitman, a lean-faced officer with a thick grey moustache. He leant against the counter and drummed his fingers on its well-polished surface.

'I'm trying to find out more about the disappearance

of Alexander Miller,' said Augusta. 'He vanished in early July 1911.'

The inspector gave an amused snort. 'You're expecting me to remember that far back?'

'No. But I'm wondering if there's anything in your records about his disappearance. Apparently his friend, John, spoke to the police about it.'

'Doesn't ring any bells with me.'

Augusta tried her best to remain patient. 'Perhaps it could be looked up in your records?'

'Now?'

Augusta glanced around the empty reception area. 'It doesn't look very busy here at the moment. Is it possible to look now?'

'At the moment it doesn't look busy. But those doors can fling open at any moment with some ruffian being marched in by my officers. It's all hands on deck when that happens.'

'Are your old files and logbooks easily accessed?' asked Augusta.

'They're stored out the back.'

'So it would take ten minutes to look up the records for July 1911?'

He blew out a sigh from beneath his grey moustache. 'Ten minutes? More like twenty.' He turned to the desk sergeant. 'See what you can find for her, Bellingham.'

Two minutes later, the desk sergeant was leafing through a logbook for July 1911. 'Miller?' he said. 'There's an entry here.'

'Let me see.' Inspector Whitman pulled the logbook across the counter. 'Where? Oh yes. There we are. You're lucky we found it so quickly, Mrs Peel. Looks like a chap by the name of John Gibson came in here on the seventeenth of July and reported Alexander Miller to be missing.'

'Did anything come of it?'

'I don't know. I'm just reading out what's written in the logbook.'

'Perhaps there's a file which relates to this entry?'

The inspector sighed and nodded at the desk sergeant who went off again. The file he returned with was thin.

'What does it say in there then, Bellingham?' asked the inspector.

The desk sergeant leafed through some sheets of paper. 'Looks like a Constable Harris visited Alexander Miller's flat and had to break in to gain entry. There was no sign of the resident inside. A search was carried out for him but he wasn't found.'

Inspector Whitman turned to Augusta. 'Does that answer your question, Mrs Peel?'

'Sort of. If Alexander Miller had been subsequently found, would there be a note about it in the file?'

'There should be. If the constable did his paperwork properly. I recall Harris was usually good with that sort of thing.'

'Where's Constable Harris now?'

'Now? I don't know. He left the Metropolitan Police to work in the country somewhere. London was clearly too much for him.' He chuckled.

'Are there any other entries in the logbook for Alexander Miller?' asked Augusta. 'Perhaps other people reported him missing too?'

'Now hold on, Mrs Peel. We haven't got all day to entertain you, you know. Like I said, those doors could fling open at any moment.'

'Do you mind looking for the first few weeks of July? That's all I ask and then I'll leave you in peace.'

'Well if you're promising to leave us in peace... go on

Bellingham.' He pushed the logbook back to the desk sergeant. 'Have a look at the rest of July.'

Augusta watched the desk sergeant turn the pages.

'Yes,' he said. 'There's another entry here.'

The inspector pulled the logbook towards him. 'The sixth of July,' he said. 'Alexander Miller reported missing by Mrs Jane Stanton.'

'Does the record say who she was?' asked Augusta.

'Mr Miller's sister.'

'So she reported her brother missing eleven days before John Gibson. Was anything done then?'

'It's difficult to say, Mrs Peel. This was ten years ago. All we've got to go on are a few pieces of paper in a file. If Mrs Stanton reported her brother missing on the sixth of July, then I don't think a great deal would have been done about it at the time. He'd only been missing a few days then. The chap could have taken himself off for a few days somewhere and it would have been a waste of our time looking for him. Your expression suggests to me I'm speaking harshly, Mrs Peel. But let me assure you we get these missing person reports on a regular basis. And most of the time the person turns up somewhere safe and well. Usually they've forgotten to tell family and friends that they were going off somewhere for a few days. So when Mrs Stanton came in, our officers wouldn't have been unduly worried. A search was clearly carried out for Mr Miller after he was reported missing the second time. As far as I can see, Mrs Peel, we did our job as well as we could.'

'Did Mrs Stanton leave an address?'

'We're not in the habit of disclosing private addresses, Mrs Peel.'

'Even when it was ten years ago?'

Inspector Whitman sighed. 'Very well. Give her the address, Bellingham.'

Chapter 7

'So you had the pleasure of meeting Inspector Whitman of D Division,' said Philip when Augusta told him and Fred about her afternoon. 'You did well to get some information from him.'

'He wasn't keen about it.'

'I'm not surprised. The man is bone idle. I've no idea how he made inspector.'

'I think it's very sad John Gibson died in an accident at Baker Street station,' said Fred.

'Yes, it's tragic,' said Augusta. 'And I've been thinking about it on my journey back here. How does someone manage to accidentally fall in front of a train? Louisa Bradshaw told me the platform was busy at the time and her brother lost his footing. But would someone really walk precariously close to the edge of the platform when it's crowded?'

'I wouldn't,' said Fred.

'Me neither.'

'It can happen,' said Philip. 'Or perhaps he jumped deliberately?'

'Mrs Bradshaw said it was an accident.'

'Perhaps it was. But some people can struggle to accept a family member would purposefully end their life. Perhaps Mrs Bradshaw wants to believe it was an accident.'

'There must have been an inquest,' said Augusta. 'The coroner would have delivered a verdict.'

'And if the verdict was an accident, what then?' said Philip.

'I'd like to find out more about the circumstances of the accident,' said Augusta. 'Was there an opportunity for someone to push Mr Gibson onto the railway line and make it look like an accident? Picture a crowded platform at a tube station and it's easy to imagine how that could have been done.'

'So you think John Gibson could have been murdered?' said Philip.

'It's a possibility, isn't it? And Alexander Miller could have been murdered too. Someone could have got rid of the pair of them.'

'But just a moment,' said Philip. 'For all we know, Alexander Miller is alive and well somewhere.'

'His sister should be able to tell me.'

'If you can find her. You have an address for her in Camden from ten years ago.'

'There's no harm in seeing if she's still there.'

'Very well.' Philip pinched his brow. 'But are you sure about this Augusta? You appear to be jumping to the worst possible conclusion about the fate of Alexander Miller and John Gibson. Perhaps there's nothing to discover? Maybe Alexander turned up again and John was a bit clumsy on a crowded tube platform. I think you're at risk of putting quite a lot of work into something which is...'

'What?'

'Something which is…. nothing after all. And these events happened in 1911.'

'I don't mind helping,' said Fred. 'I can look in the newspaper archive at the library and see if there are any reports on John Gibson's inquest.'

'That would be very helpful, Fred,' said Augusta.

Philip groaned and shook his head. 'Look at the influence you have, Augusta. You've even got Fred doing some sleuthing now.'

Augusta and Fred exchanged a smile.

'So what would you do about this case, Philip?' Augusta asked.

'Case? I don't think it can be called that yet. You've got a man who went missing but may have turned up again. And another man who died in an accident. The two men were friends, but there's nothing to suggest the accident was connected to the disappearance. It's not really a case.'

'So you would forget about it?'

'Personally I would. But you found the letter, Augusta, so I suppose that's piqued your interest. And I know what you're like. You don't stop until you find an answer. So…'

'I'm wasting my time?'

'Possibly.' He smiled. 'Or possibly not.'

Chapter 8

THE FOLLOWING MORNING, Augusta travelled by tube to Camden. The address for Alexander Miller's sister was a small, terraced house on a scruffy, narrow street situated between a railway line and the Regent's Canal.

'They moved,' said the sallow-faced woman who answered the door.

'Do you know where to?' Augusta asked.

'Baker Street.'

'Do you know which number?'

'No.'

The door was closed on her.

Augusta decided to try her luck at Alexander Miller's former flat. Number 15, Baker Street.

The address was at the lower end of Baker Street, close to Portman Square. The street was lined with tall, brown-brick Georgian buildings with large sash windows. The ground storeys were occupied by everyday shops and tradespeople. It wasn't a fashionable street, like some in the West End, but it was fairly smart and respectable.

'Excuse me,' said a bespectacled man with a camera. 'Can you tell me where I might find number 221b?'

'Sherlock Holmes's address, you mean?'

'Yes!'

'I'm afraid it doesn't exist.'

His face fell. 'So that's why I can't find it.'

'Yes. The address is fictional. You do realise Sherlock Holmes is fictional too?'

'Of course! But I didn't realise Conan Doyle made up the address.' He glanced around sadly. 'Do you know which house he based it on?'

'I'm afraid not,' said Augusta. 'Perhaps you could look around and decide for yourself which one it could have been?'

The man gave a grunt and walked away.

Augusta found number 15. It was a hairdresser's shop with four floors above it. Little brass plaques next to a door at the side of the shop had the surnames of the building occupants on them. Augusta was pleased to see the name Stanton. This was the surname of Alexander Miller's sister and her husband.

There was no Miller on the other plaques. Did this mean Alexander's sister and husband had moved into Alexander Miller's flat?

Inside the building, Augusta climbed three flights of stairs to a smart green door with the name Stanton on it. She took in a breath, knocked, and waited.

A lady about the same age as Augusta opened the door. She had sharp, regular features and wavy hair streaked with steel grey. There was a hint of wariness about her.

'My name is Augusta Peel. I'm a private investigator,' she said. 'I also own a second-hand bookshop.' She smiled, aware the two statements didn't match very well. 'Am I speaking with Jane Stanton?'

An eyebrow raised at the mention of her name. 'Yes. What do you want?'

'I found a letter which discussed your brother's disappearance.'

'Alexander?' Her face softened. 'I suppose you had better come in. But this can't take long, I'm afraid. I have to go out shortly.'

Augusta followed her into a flat which was more spacious than she had been expecting. They passed doors of various rooms as Jane Stanton led her to a sitting room with two large windows overlooking Baker Street. It was a clean, tidy room with modern furniture. Mrs Stanton was clearly someone who avoided trinkets and ornaments. She gestured for Augusta to take a seat on a brown leather sofa. Then she sat in an armchair, her back stiff and straight. She wore a cream silk blouse with pearls and a long maroon skirt.

Augusta took in a breath and tried to put herself at ease.

'So what's this letter you mention?' asked Mrs Stanton.

'I found it in a book I was repairing for my bookshop. It was written by John Gibson and he sent it to his sister Louisa Bradshaw. Do you know the names?'

'I can recall John. Alexander talked about him from time to time.'

'When I read the letter, I wondered if Alexander Miller was ever found again.'

Mrs Stanton's lips pursed. 'He wasn't.'

'So you never found out what happened to him?'

'No.'

Augusta said nothing, hoping Mrs Stanton would fill the silence. She fingered the string of pearls around her neck and eventually continued. 'It was as if Alexander had disappeared into thin air. Some harm must have come to him, but I don't know what or when. The police weren't much help. I reported him missing a few days after he vanished, but they told me there wasn't a lot they could do. They said he could be just about anywhere. I think they made some inquiries with local doctors and hospitals to find out if he had been injured and found somewhere. But they did little else. They even suggested he'd met a young lady and gone off with her. They were no help at all. And then I received a letter which was supposedly from him.'

'Supposedly?'

'I say that because it didn't seem like he'd written it. It was typewritten and said he'd moved to the north of England to start a new life and didn't want to be contacted.'

'Did your brother usually write his letters on a typewriter?'

'No. My brother didn't write letters to me very often, but they were always handwritten.'

'So you don't believe the letter came from him?'

'No. I think someone else wrote it. The wording of the letter didn't sound like the way he spoke.'

'Did you show the letter to the police?'

'Yes, but they didn't do much with it.'

'The person who wrote that letter must have known what had happened to your brother.'

'Yes, they must have done.'

'And therefore something criminal must have occurred. I can't believe the police did nothing about it.'

'They tried. But what could they do? It was just a type-written letter with no address on it. Anyone could have sent it.'

'Do you still have the letter?' Augusta asked.

Mrs Stanton nodded.

'Where did the postmark say it had been posted from?'

'Birmingham.' She sighed. 'And that's where the trail goes cold. So I don't know what can be done about it. Nothing I suppose.' A pause followed before she spoke again. 'You're a private detective, you say?'

'Yes. And your brother's disappearance has intrigued me since I read about it. I don't understand how a young man can vanish like that. I visited you today hoping that you'd since discovered what had happened to him. But for him to have been missing for ten years...'

'I no longer hold out any hope he's still alive. If he was, then I would have heard from him. A few years ago we applied to a court to have him declared dead. It's possible to do that once seven years have passed since someone went missing. It was a very difficult thing to do, but it was the only way the probate could be settled.'

'And this flat was once his flat?'

'Yes. It legally belongs to me and my husband now, but we moved in here a few months after Alexander went missing. I couldn't bear to see it sitting empty.'

Having visited the Stanton's previous address in Camden, Augusta knew this flat was superior in both size and location.

'Apparently, John Gibson reported Alexander's disappearance to the police, too,' said Augusta.

'Yes, he called on me when he was looking for Alexander. He persuaded the police to break in the door of this flat to check if Alexander was here. He wasn't, of course.'

'Did you know John Gibson died five months later in an accident at Baker Street station?'

'Did he? How awful. I didn't know that. Life can be cruel sometimes.'

'And so can people, Mrs Stanton. I want to find the

person who sent you that letter pretending to be your brother.'

Jane Stanton gave her a thin smile. 'Well, that's very admirable, Mrs Peel. But it was ten years ago. I'm afraid you don't have any hope of succeeding.'

Chapter 9

'I HAD some success in the library yesterday evening,' said Fred when Augusta arrived back at her shop. 'I had to work quickly, though, because it was almost closing time. My notes are quite scribbled.'

'But you managed to find a report of John Gibson's inquest?'

'Yes. A few, actually.'

'Excellent!'

A customer entered the shop. He was a tall man with thick-lensed spectacles. He peered myopically at the shelves and Augusta went to his assistance. After he had left with a book about Britain's cathedrals, she went back to Fred and his notebook.

'It happened in November 1911,' he said. 'There was quite a lot of detail in the reports. Interestingly, the witnesses differed in their opinions about what had happened. Everyone agreed the platform was crowded at the time because it was morning rush hour. John Gibson was going to his job at the Great Western Railway headquarters at Paddington station.

He travelled there every day on the Metropolitan Railway from Baker Street station. One witness said he'd seen Mr Gibson on the track as the train was pulling into the station.'

'Oh no.' Augusta shuddered.

'Another witness said he'd purposefully jumped in front of the train as it had arrived.'

'Really?'

'And another witness said they hadn't seen him fall in front of the train, but he'd heard people on the platform screaming when it happened. A station master gave evidence and described how busy the platform could get at that time in the morning. He said if someone was trying to walk along the platform, they were forced to do so on the platform edge. It was therefore easy for them to be accidentally nudged onto the tracks. The train driver said he saw Mr Gibson jump.'

'Goodness. So it's difficult to determine exactly what happened.'

'The coroner questioned Mr Gibson's father and a friend who both testified that he'd been happy and had no thoughts of suicide.'

'So he couldn't have jumped as the train driver and one of the witnesses suggested.'

'The coroner gave the verdict of death by misadventure.'

'An accident, as John Gibson's sister told me,' said Augusta. 'But the word "misadventure" suggests there was some fault on Mr Gibson's part.'

'Perhaps it describes the fact he went too close to the platform edge?'

'Yes, I suppose that's right. But it sounds like he had little choice if the platform was crowded.'

Augusta fed some seed to Sparky as she thought.

'Did the coroner discuss the possibility Mr Gibson had been pushed?' she asked Fred.

'It wasn't mentioned in the reports I read.'

'But it's still possible, don't you think? A deliberate push may not be obvious when there are a lot of people on the platform. It could have been a slight nudge, couldn't it? If he was standing close to the platform edge, it may not have taken much to make him overbalance.'

'I agree. But if the platform was very busy, then it could have been an accident, couldn't it? Someone could have knocked into him.'

'But no one admitted they did,' said Augusta.

'No. Perhaps they didn't want to because they were worried it would land them in trouble. No witness says they saw him being knocked into.'

'It's interesting that the witness accounts vary so much, isn't it? You'd think the presence of many people at the time would have ensured an accurate account would be established. But it seems the opposite is true. People reported what they thought they saw. I think it's almost impossible to establish exactly what happened.'

Augusta heard footsteps on the staircase and turned to see Philip making his way down. His progress was slow because he needed the aid of a walking stick.

'Augusta!' he said. 'Did you find Alexander Miller's sister?'

'Yes. She lives in his former flat on Baker Street.'

'Really?' Philip made his way to the counter. 'And did her brother ever turn up?'

'No.'

'Oh dear, that's sad news. So she never found out what happened to him?'

'She received a letter after his disappearance claiming

to be from him. But it was typewritten, and she believes someone else wrote it.'

'Can she prove it came from someone else?'

'She said Alexander never typed his letters. And she said the wording of the letter didn't sound like him. She's quite convinced it wasn't from him. And she would know.'

'Did she show the letter to the police at the time?'

'Yes, but ultimately their inquiries led to nothing.'

'That's a shame. Does she still have the letter?'

'Yes. And the fact she received it suggests someone knew what happened to her brother. I think it must be the person responsible for his disappearance.'

'Unless it was someone playing a prank. It's not unusual for strange people to send weird letters when something like this happens.'

'I think it would be useful for someone from the police to get involved again. Do you think you could persuade a former colleague to pay her a visit and ask about the letter?'

'If the police get involved again, then it will come under the remit of Inspector Whitman at Crawford Place station. You've met him and you've seen what he's like, Augusta.'

'Could you try speaking to him?'

'I can't imagine him wanting to spend any time on this. See it from his point of view. His division looked into this ten years ago and got nowhere with it. Why would it be any different a second time?'

'But would you at least try?'

'Alright then. I'll try. But I can't promise I'll get anywhere with it.'

'I'm sure you'll be able to convince them.'

'I don't know about that. I've failed to convince the War Office that Walter Ferguson is up to no good.'

'Oh no,' said Augusta. 'You spoke to someone there?'

'Yes, I spoke to a civil servant and explained that I suspect someone working there has passed information from confidential files to a news reporter. The first thing he did was ask me for evidence. And that's where I became stuck. Because I don't actually have any evidence that it's happened. But if Walter Ferguson knows your real name, Augusta, he can only have got it from your file at the War Office.'

'Perhaps he doesn't have it after all. Perhaps he's bluffing.'

'He could be. And that's the difficulty we have. He's threatening to reveal this information about you. But does he really have it? Or is he just trying to make you feel uncomfortable?'

'I think he's trying to make me feel uncomfortable either way. He's a weird man. I'm astonished no one can do anything about him.'

Philip sighed. 'I can have a word with the editor, Mr Baker, at the *London Weekly Chronicle*. We met him during our previous investigation didn't we? But he seems a fairly ineffectual man. I don't think he can keep Walter Ferguson under control. So I'm a bit stuck at the moment. I think the War Office would do something about it if we were able to tell them which employee it was who gave Walter Ferguson the information. But we don't know for certain that it actually happened.'

'Could the police be persuaded to interview Ferguson and get the name from him?' asked Fred.

'It's possible,' said Philip. 'But the police need a valid reason to interview him. Obviously there's a suspicion that he's paid an employee at the War Office for confidential information. But there's no evidence at all. I'll visit Mr

Baker the editor next and see where that gets us. Walter Ferguson shouldn't be able to do this.'

Chapter 10

A NEWS REPORTER called at Augusta's bookshop the next day. 'I write for the *Daily London News*,' he said. 'And I've heard all about the hidden letter from Mrs Bradshaw! She telephoned our newspaper suggesting it would be an interesting story and I've just spent an hour with her. She suggested I speak to you as well. I'm writing an article about how the letter has been found again after all these years. Do you mind being interviewed about it?'

Augusta's encounter with Walter Ferguson had left her wary of news reporters. 'It depends on what you want to ask me,' she replied.

'I'm just interested in how you found the letter.'

'It was in a book which had been left in a box of other books on the doorstep of my shop.'

'*The Invisible Man* by H. G. Wells. Am I right?'

'Yes. Surely Mrs Bradshaw has told you everything you need to know?'

'She's been very helpful. But I'd like to speak to all parties involved. I'm planning to interview Mr Miller's sister, Mrs Stanton, next.'

Augusta couldn't imagine Mrs Stanton being overjoyed by his visit.

'So what did you think when you came across the letter?' he asked.

'I was quite surprised because it was ten years old.' Augusta answered more of the reporter's mundane questions, then told him she had work to be getting on with.

'Of course. Do you mind if a photographer calls in later to take your photograph?'

'Yes, I do mind.'

His face fell. 'You don't want your photograph in the *Daily London News*?'

'No. I really don't.'

'We can give your shop a mention. You might get a few new customers out of it.'

'I'm quite alright. Thank you.'

'Very well. Thank you for your time, Mrs Peel. The article should be published the day after tomorrow. Keep an eye out for it!'

Chapter 11

PHILIP PERSUADED Inspector Whitman to send a constable to Mrs Stanton and have another look at the letter.

'It's young Constable Simpson,' Philip told Augusta. 'I know his father well, we worked together at the Yard. I've had a word with Simpson and he's happy for you to accompany him.'

'Really?'

'And it will probably help because you've already met Mrs Stanton. Your presence might put her at ease.'

'I don't know about that. She's not the sort of woman I can imagine being at ease.'

Augusta met Constable Simpson outside number 15, Baker Street. He was slender with pale, pimpled skin and looked no older than twenty. Inspector Whitman had clearly offered up his most junior officer.

Jane Stanton was unimpressed when she answered the door to them. 'I don't understand this interest all of a sudden,' she said. 'Nothing has happened for ten years and now I've got detectives, reporters and police officers on my doorstep.'

Once they were seated in her sitting room, Constable Simpson asked to see the letter which Mrs Stanton had received after her brother's disappearance.

'Very well.' She left the room to fetch it and returned a few moments later. 'I don't know what you'll be able to do with it, but here it is.' She handed it to the constable. He examined the envelope then scrutinised the letter inside it.

'And you're sure this letter wasn't from your brother?' he asked.

'Yes. Alexander never typed his letters, and the wording is not how he spoke. I think someone typed this letter because they were unable to forge his handwriting.'

Constable Simpson nodded. 'That makes sense. By typing the letter, the problem of forged handwriting is solved. This letter suggests your brother decided to start a new life in the north of England. Was that something he mentioned to you beforehand?'

'No never. He never expressed any intention to start a new life elsewhere. And he wouldn't have done. He seemed happy here in London. There was no reason for him to leave and start a new life elsewhere.'

'Do you know what the state of his finances was?'

'Finances?' Mrs Stanton clutched her pearls. Augusta was surprised by the alarm on her face. Then she appeared to recover herself. 'His finances were fine. He had no financial worries.'

'Do you have any family members living up north?'

'None. And with all due respect to you, Constable, I went through all of this with the police ten years ago. When you were still in short trousers. I have nothing new to tell you, I'm afraid.'

Augusta found her manner odd. Even though a decade

had passed, surely Jane Stanton would still want to do what she could to find her brother?

Constable Simpson seemed unbothered by Mrs Stanton's caustic remark about his age. 'Can you think of anyone who would have wanted to harm your brother?' he asked.

'No. I can't think of anyone at all. He was completely harmless. He wouldn't have hurt anyone. Not intentionally anyway…' she trailed off and fidgeted with her pearls.

'Are you saying he hurt someone unintentionally?' asked Augusta.

'Well he was involved in an accident about a year before he disappeared.'

'What sort of accident?' asked Constable Simpson.

'He collided with someone when he was riding his bicycle. Unfortunately, the man died a few days later in hospital. It wasn't Alexander's fault, the man just stepped out in front of him.'

'Where did this happen?'

'In Finchley. The man was called Mr Connolly. He'd been drinking all afternoon in The Queen's Head on Regent's Park Road. When he staggered out of the pub, he wasn't concentrating on his surroundings. He stepped out into the road and collided with Alexander. It was at the bottom of a hill, so Alexander was going at quite a speed. Alexander was hurt too, he broke his arm. And he hurt his back as well.

'The inquest ruled it was an accident. Although it's quite obvious Mr Connolly was at fault. He was under the influence of drink and so his judgement was impaired. Mr Connolly's family pointed the finger at Alexander though. They said he had been cycling dangerously. He had been riding down a hill, that's all there is to it.'

'Why did they think Alexander was at fault?' asked Augusta.

'Because they didn't want to accept that their husband, father and brother was careless enough to step into the path of a bicycle. They were upset about it, and they wanted someone to blame. So that's why they blamed Alexander.'

'It must have been very difficult for everyone.'

'It was. Then a week after the inquest, Mr Connolly's brother called on Alexander and said some very hurtful things to him.'

'Oh dear,' said Augusta. 'Did he threaten him?'

'Probably. I'm not sure exactly what he said. Alexander didn't like talking about it because it upset him. The Connolly family said Alexander should be tried for murder. They kept calling him a murderer. Well that just wasn't the truth at all. So it was all very unpleasant.

'Alexander was absolutely distraught about the accident. He struggled to cope with the fact that he had accidentally ended someone's life.'

'So the Connolly family had a motive for harming your brother,' said Augusta.

'Yes. But I don't think I've ever seriously thought they could have been behind his disappearance. And besides, none of them would have been able to type a letter pretending to be from him. They were barely literate.'

'The letter was posted in Birmingham,' said Constable Simpson. 'But the sender of this letter claimed Mr Miller had moved up north. Birmingham isn't north, it's in the Midlands.'

'Yes, I know,' said Mrs Stanton.

'So it begs the question why this letter was posted in Birmingham,' said the constable. 'Birmingham is close enough to London that someone could have travelled by train there, posted this letter, then returned to London within the same day.'

'Are you thinking the sender of this letter could have been from London and tried to disguise that fact by posting the letter from Birmingham?' Augusta asked.

'Yes I am thinking that. And it supports Mrs Stanton's idea that the letter is a forgery. If Mr Miller really had sent it because he had moved up north, then you would have expected it to have been posted up north.'

'But where does all this talk get us?' said Mrs Stanton with a sigh. 'Nowhere. Ten years have passed since the letter was written.'

'The passage of time can be useful,' said Augusta. 'Perhaps someone has made a confession to someone else during that time. I believe that at least one person knew what happened to Alexander. What if more people know now?'

'If they do, they're not exactly volunteering the information are they?' said Mrs Stanton.

'With your permission, Mrs Stanton, I would like to keep hold of this letter,' said Constable Simpson. 'I'm quite convinced your brother didn't write it. I shall speak to my superiors about it. I can't promise that a full investigation will be carried out again, but I'll do what I can.'

'Fine. Do what you will.' She gave him a dismissive wave.

The gesture angered Augusta. Constable Simpson was keen and doing his best to help. But Jane Stanton's indifference was bordering on rudeness. Was it her usual nature, or did she have something to hide?

Chapter 12

'SPARKY, you look more handsome every time I see you,' said Lady Hereford. 'You're ageing remarkably well.'

She fed the canary some seed as she sat in her bath chair by the counter in Augusta's shop. Sparky belonged to Lady Hereford, but Augusta looked after him for her.

'How old is Sparky?' asked Augusta.

'Now there's a question. I acquired him as my husband's health began to decline. I think he must be five years old now. Equivalent to a fifty-year-old person.'

'Really?'

'I can't be completely sure. I think canaries can live ten or twelve years. Perhaps he's more like a forty-year-old. Either way, he's looking wonderful for it.'

'He is.'

'Now tell me what you've been up to, Augusta.'

'Just the usual things. Running the shop. With Fred's help, of course.' She gave Fred a smile. 'And I found an old letter.'

'An old letter?'

'There's an article in the *Daily London News* today which explains it all,' said Fred.

'You're in the newspaper again, Augusta?' asked Lady Hereford.

'I'm mentioned in a couple of sentences, but thankfully that's all. They wanted to take my photograph, but I refused.'

'You refused? If I'd been asked, then I'd have happily had my photograph in the newspaper! You're too modest, Augusta. So what's so interesting about the old letter you found?'

'I'll summarise the news article for you, Lady Hereford,' said Fred. 'The headline reads, "Long Lost Letter Reopens The Case Of The Missing Man."'

'Goodness. Who's the missing man?'

'Alexander Miller,' said Fred. 'The article here says Mrs Louisa Bradshaw was surprised to receive a letter which had originally been sent to her ten years ago. The letter was found in a copy of *The Invisible Man* by H. G. Wells which had found its way into a second-hand bookshop belonging to Mrs Augusta Peel. When Mrs Peel found the letter inside the book, she decided to return it to its original recipient.'

'What a good idea, Augusta!' said Lady Hereford.

'Mrs Bradshaw said she was delighted to see the letter again and couldn't remember putting it in the book,' continued Fred. 'However, she recalled lending the book to a friend during the war. The book was then found in a box of books left anonymously outside Mrs Peel's shop last week. Mrs Bradshaw said the letter described a mystery. It was written by her late brother, John Gibson, who wrote about the disappearance of his friend Alexander Miller. Mr Miller was twenty-five and worked as a clerk in the accounts department at the Great Western Railway's headquarters at Paddington station. He was last seen at his place of work on 1st July 1911. He had been due to go on a cycling excursion with Mr Gibson the following weekend but didn't turn up.

'Mrs Bradshaw says her brother made some attempts to find his friend, but he tragically lost his life in an accident at Baker Street tube station in November 1911.

'Alexander Miller's sister, Jane Stanton, lives with her husband in her brother's former flat on Baker Street. She says she received a letter which had supposedly been written by her brother a few weeks after he vanished. The letter claimed he had moved to the north to start a new life. Mrs Stanton believes the letter was a forgery and hadn't been written by her brother.'

'Good grief,' said Lady Hereford. 'So who wrote it?'

'That's what I'd like to find out,' said Augusta.

'Mrs Stanton thinks her brother may no longer be alive because she feels sure he would have contacted her,' continued Fred. 'She says having some knowledge of what had happened to him would bring her solace. Even if it was confirmation he has died.'

'How very sad,' said Lady Hereford. 'The absence of information must be the hardest thing of all.'

'And then there's an appeal for information at the end of the article,' said Fred. 'It says: "Do you know what happened to Alexander Miller? Anyone with information is encouraged to telephone or write to this newspaper. The *Daily London News* is offering a monetary reward of five hundred pounds to anyone who can provide evidence confirming Mr Miller's fate."'

'Five hundred pounds!' said Lady Hereford. 'That's a lot of money to tempt someone with.'

'There are three photographs printed alongside the

article,' said Fred. 'There's a picture of Mrs Bradshaw, a picture of Mrs Stanton and a picture of Mr Miller.'

'Let's see what he looked like,' said Lady Hereford.

Fred passed the newspaper to her. Augusta had already read the article and seen the photograph of Alexander Miller. He was dark-haired and had the same sharp features as his sister. He was posing with his bicycle and wore a tweed jacket with matching knee-length trousers, long socks, and a sports cap.

'Alas, there's no photograph of Augusta to look at,' said Fred with a smile.

'But never mind,' said Augusta. 'You have the real person here with you now! It will be interesting to find out if anybody contacts the newspaper with information.'

'With five hundred pounds on offer, I'm sure they'll hear from a lot of people,' said Fred. 'And they'll probably receive all sorts of weird and wonderful stories.'

'Yes, I think you could be right, Fred,' said Lady Hereford. 'People will probably make up any old nonsense in the hope they can get their hands on the money.'

'Hopefully someone who knows something will get in touch,' said Augusta. 'I didn't particularly want to speak to the news reporter, but I think it's good this article has been published and the public is being reminded about Alexander Miller.'

'They need to find out if anyone wanted to harm him,' said Lady Hereford.

'I agree,' said Augusta. 'And I heard an interesting story from his sister this morning. She told me and Constable Simpson that her brother was involved in a bicycle accident in which a man died.' She explained the incident with Mr Connolly.

'And Mr Miller went missing a year after that happened?' said Fred.

'That's right.'

'Would the Connolly family really have waited a year to take their revenge?'

'I don't know, Fred. I'd like to learn some more about them before I can say.'

'I can make another trip to look at the old newspapers in Holborn Library,' said Fred. 'I'm sure the bicycle accident in Finchley would have been written about at the time.'

'Thank you, Fred. We might find out something useful.'

'Have you got Fred doing detective work as well now, Augusta?' said Lady Hereford.

'I didn't order him to,' said Augusta. 'He volunteered.'

'And I enjoy it,' said Fred with a grin. 'Mysteries like this draw you in.'

Chapter 13

'So now you're famous, Jane,' said Robert Stanton as he read the *Daily London News* before dinner that evening.

'Not famous, exactly.' She gave a nervous laugh, knowing he had disapproved of her speaking to the news reporter about her brother, Alexander.

Her husband folded the newspaper up and tossed it onto the coffee table. 'I still don't see what you hoped to achieve by having all the details printed in the newspaper.'

'We discussed this, didn't we, Robert? I didn't give the news reporter much information at all. He asked me a few questions, and that was it.'

'And took your photograph.'

'A photographer came to do that.'

'And there you are grinning away in the newspaper now. Your moment of fame.'

She laughed again, doing her best to lift his mood. 'It's not fame, Robert. It's just…'

'Just what?' He scowled at her. He had a red, square face and cold grey eyes.

She felt herself faltering under his gaze and looked away. 'It just allows Alexander to be remembered.'

'You can remember him without speaking to the newspapers. Why did the reporter call here in the first place? Was it because that private detective woman called round? I forget her name, now.'

'Mrs Peel.'

'Mrs Peel. Did she contact the papers?'

'No, the reporter told me it was the sister, Louisa Bradshaw. She's the woman the letter had been sent to.'

'Why did she do it?'

'She must have thought it was an interesting story.'

'But she's not the one with the brother who went missing, is she? You're the one most affected by this, Jane. And I don't think it's right that it's all out in the open like this. I blame that Mrs Peel for starting it all off. And she's got the police involved!'

'They were hopeless the first time round, and they'll be just as hopeless again. You should have seen the constable, he didn't look a day over twelve.'

'It doesn't matter how old he was. The police are involved, Jane, and that's quite unnecessary.'

'I've told them they won't get anywhere with it. Too much time has passed.'

'So why do you insist on speaking to them then? Just tell them to go away the next time they call round.' Robert got up and poured himself a large whisky. 'What does Mrs Peel want out of this?'

'She has a notion she can find out what happened to Alexander. She came across the letter and initially called here because she was interested to find out if Alexander's disappearance had ever been solved.'

'I think it's strange.' He took a gulp of whisky. 'If I

found a letter like that, I wouldn't go around knocking on doors and speaking to people about it. She upset you.'

'She didn't upset me.'

'Yes, she did. I can tell she did. I know when you're upset, Jane.'

'How? I don't feel upset.'

'I can tell by your gestures. I know when you're anxious.'

She felt herself stiffen. Her husband made her more anxious than anyone else she knew.

'That woman put you on edge,' continued Robert. 'I don't like her asking questions.'

'Why?'

'Did you tell her the truth?'

'What do you mean?'

'Did you tell Mrs Peel that the last time you saw your brother was when you had that horrendous argument with him?'

'No, of course I didn't tell her that. And I don't like to think about it now. You know how awful that made me feel.'

'And what if she discovers you lied to her? What then? She's working with the police. You know what they're like when they discover you haven't been honest.'

'I was honest. But the argument isn't relevant.'

He gave a dry laugh and refilled his whisky glass. 'That's what you think, Jane. Just you wait until they learn about the argument.'

'They won't.'

'It's far better to refuse to talk about these things from the outset. The moment you try to pretend that everything was fine between you and your brother, then you're covering something up. And it's too late now, you've said too much.'

'Mrs Peel won't find out about it.'

'She's a private detective, Jane. Who knows what she's planning?'

'She's only a part-time private detective. She told me she runs a second-hand bookshop.'

'Which one?'

'I don't know. She mentioned it's in Bloomsbury.'

'So this woman who runs a bookshop and does a bit of work on the side as a private detective turned up on our doorstep asking you about your brother who went missing ten years ago. There's something odd happening here. Someone must have said something.'

'No. It was because she found the letter.'

'How can you be sure? Did you see the letter?'

'No.'

'I think someone has stirred something up.' Robert drained his glass and paced the sitting room. 'Everything has been nice and quiet for ten years and now this. Who had that letter before Mrs Peel supposedly found it?'

'I don't know. It was in a book, wasn't it?'

'I think someone deliberately ensured Mrs Peel came across that letter. How else could it have found its way into the hands of a private detective?'

'I don't know. Shall we have dinner?'

'Don't attempt to change the subject, Jane!'

She sat back, silenced.

A horrible sensation of dread lurched in her stomach. She felt as though she had done something wrong. She wished Robert would forget about it all. But she knew he wasn't going to.

Chapter 14

'My library visit after work yesterday was worthwhile,' said Fred. 'I managed to find quite a bit of information about Alexander Miller's bicycle accident.'

'You did? Well done!' said Augusta. 'You're proving yourself to be a useful detective.'

Fred looked bashful as he pulled his notebook out of his pocket. 'I wrote everything down in here. Oh, I can hear someone coming down the stairs. I'll tell you all about it later.'

'Thank you, Fred. I'm looking forward to it.'

A tall, broad man with grey hair came into view. He was followed by Philip.

'Augusta! Fred!' said Philip. 'I'd like to introduce you to Mr Ramsden. I'm doing some work for him.'

'It's a pleasure to meet you both.' Mr Ramsden strode towards them, hand outstretched. He held a trilby hat in his other hand and wore a smart suit. A thick, gold watch chain hung across the front of his waistcoat.

'I asked Mr Fisher about this delightful-looking shop,' he said after he had shaken their hands. 'I love bookshops.

And what a wonderful surprise it was to discover that the shop is owned by a friend of Mr Fisher's. Better still, there is direct access from his office above!'

He chuckled, deepening the laughter lines at the corners of his sparkling blue eyes.

'I told Mr Ramsden he's welcome to look around,' said Philip.

'Of course,' said Augusta. 'Very welcome indeed.'

'It's a pleasure to meet you, Mrs Peel,' said Mr Ramsden. 'This really is an impressive place you have here.'

'I'm not sure I'd describe it as impressive,' said Augusta, embarrassed by the flattery. 'It's just some second-hand books.'

'Mr Fisher tells me you repair the books yourself.'

'Yes. Many of these books would have been otherwise thrown away and I think that's a great shame. Especially as some of them are first editions and can be quite valuable if they're well looked after.'

'Absolutely. I do enjoy a bit of reading myself. I think I shall take some time to peruse your shelves if you don't mind, Mrs Peel? I could do with some new books for my library.'

'Of course.'

'If you feel our business is concluded for today, Mr Ramsden, then I shall leave you in the capable hands of Mrs Peel,' said Philip.

'Absolutely,' said Mr Ramsden. 'And don't worry about looking after me here, Mrs Peel. I'll have a look around and select some books which look good. I'll let you know when I'm ready to purchase them.'

'Very well,' said Augusta. 'Take all the time you need.'

Philip returned to his office and Mr Ramsden eventually bought five books. 'I'll be back,' he said when Augusta thanked him for his custom. 'A detective and a bookshop all in the same building. Simply perfect! He's very professional, isn't he, Mr Fisher? He told me he used to work for Scotland Yard.'

'Yes, they were foolish to lose him,' said Augusta. 'He was a good detective for them. But now he can work for himself, and I think he prefers it that way.'

'Good for him! Until next time, Mrs Peel!' He put his trilby on his head and went on his way.

Augusta dashed up to Philip's office as soon as Mr Ramsden had left.

Philip laughed. 'I know why you're here, Augusta! You want to know what sort of work Mr Ramsden wants me to do for him.'

'I do.' She sat in the chair across the desk from him. 'Is that nosy of me?'

'Very nosy. And I don't think it's appropriate for me to discuss my clients' business with other people. But I think I can trust you, Augusta.'

'Good. So who is he?'

'Mr Ramsden is the director of a pharmaceutical firm, Hodgson Medicines.'

'And what work are you doing for him?'

'To be honest with you, I wish it were more interesting than it actually is. He's asked me to watch his wife for him. He suspects she's having an extramarital affair.'

'So that means you have to follow her about?'

'Yes, it does. I need to make a note of where she goes and who she meets with.'

'That could become tedious quite quickly.'

'You're not wrong, Augusta. But this sort of work is commonplace for private detectives, so I have to expect it. I've told him I'll work on the case for a month. It's not the sort of thing I want to be working on indefinitely. If Mrs Ramsden is having an affair, then I feel sure I'll find the evidence within a month.'

'And if you don't find any evidence?'

'Then it means she's either not having an affair, or she's very good at hiding it.'

'You might find evidence within a few days.'

'I might indeed. Although I'll be happy if this work takes a little longer. Mr Ramsden is paying me very well for it.'

'That's excellent news, Philip. Perhaps you could use the funds to buy some more books for your bookshelf?' Augusta eyed the solitary book on it and smiled.

Chapter 15

'I FOUND this silver cufflink on the shop floor earlier,' said Fred. He pulled it out of his pocket. 'D. C. it says on it.'

He and Augusta sat in her workshop once the bookshop had closed for the day.

'Let's have a look.' She peered at it. 'It looks like a nice silver cufflink, too. D. C. What could those letters stand for?'

'David Cartwright.'

'Who's he?'

'I don't know.' Fred laughed. 'I made it up.'

'Well it could belong to someone with that name. We'll keep it safe and I'm sure David will come back for it.'

'I'll put it in our lost property box behind the counter.'

'Thank you. Now what did you find out about the accident between Alexander Miller and Arthur Connolly?

'It happened in the summer of 1910,' said Fred. 'Mr Miller was returning home from an appointment in Finchley and was cycling down Regent's Park Road. It was the stretch of road which runs downhill from Finchley railway station to the crossroads. Do you know it? Where

Gravel Hill and East End Road meet Regent's Park Road. The Queen's Head public house is on the corner of East End Road and Regent's Park Road.'

'I don't know the area well,' said Augusta. Finchley was a parish north of London which had grown rapidly since the Victorian era. She estimated Alexander Miller could have cycled the route between there and Baker Street in under an hour.

'I've been to Finchley a few times,' said Fred. 'So I can picture the location of the accident. It was a summer evening in June when Mr Miller collided with Mr Connolly who had just left the pub. It was about half-past eight and still light. The reports say the collision sent both men sprawling into the road. Mr Miller suffered a broken arm and cuts and bruises. Mr Connolly knocked his head on a kerbstone.'

'Oh dear.' Augusta winced.

'They were both taken to the Hampstead General Hospital,' said Fred. 'Mr Miller was able to go home two days later, but Mr Connolly unfortunately died there from his injuries. He was fifty-one years old.'

'How sad.'

'I found reports of the inquest into Mr Connolly's death,' continued Fred. 'Lots of witnesses were called, including Mr Connolly's friends who he had been drinking with in the pub that day. They had gone to the pub after work and stayed there for three hours. Mr Connolly's friends said he was under the influence of drink when he left the pub, having consumed between six and eight pints of beer.

'A lady who was walking on the pavement at the time of the accident said she saw Mr Connolly leave the pub and she could tell from his unsteady gait that he had consumed a lot of drink. She said he looked up and down the road as if considering whether to cross it. But then staggered on a bit before actually stepping into the road. She said when he first looked up and down the road, there was no sign of Mr Miller. But about a minute later, she could see Mr Miller cycling down the road. He was moving fast because he was travelling downhill. The witness thought nothing more of it until Mr Connolly unexpectedly stepped out in front of Mr Miller. He hadn't looked in Mr Miller's direction at all. She said Mr Miller was going very fast and suggested he could have slowed his bicycle a little when he saw the pedestrian so close to the edge of the road.'

'Did Alexander Miller give evidence?' asked Augusta.

'Yes. He said he hadn't expected Mr Connolly to step out in front of him. He said he applied the brakes, but it was already too late. Apparently, there was nothing he could have done to avoid Mr Connolly. The lady witness said the accident happened so quickly that Mr Connolly probably hadn't even realised what had happened. She helped both men immediately after the accident, as did some motorists and a few people who'd been on a passing tram. Mr Miller had injured his arm, but he was able to get to his feet. Mr Connolly's condition concerned everyone because the accident had knocked him unconscious. An ambulance was called, and he was taken to the hospital. The doctors at the hospital did what they could for him, but sadly, he succumbed to the head injury. He never regained consciousness.'

'How awful,' said Augusta. 'I'm astonished Mr Miller wasn't more seriously hurt.'

'The coroner ruled the death as an accident. He said it was quite apparent that Mr Connolly had not been paying due care and attention when attempting to cross the road.

He said his judgement was impaired after drinking a significant amount of alcohol.'

'An awful accident which you can only hope you never end up involved in yourself. There's not a lot that can be done about it, is there? I can understand why the Connolly family were upset, but Alexander Miller doesn't appear to have been at fault. Perhaps he was going a little too fast on his bicycle, and perhaps he should have paid more attention to the man who was stumbling around on the pavement near the pub. But even so, you don't expect someone to step out in front of you like that. It could have happened to anyone travelling along that road, whether they were on a bicycle or in a motor car.'

'I agree,' said Fred.

'But it makes you wonder, doesn't it?'

'Wonder what?'

'If Alexander Miller's disappearance could be connected to this accident.'

Chapter 16

'I THINK it's possible the two incidents could be connected,' said Philip when Augusta discussed the Finchley accident with him the following morning.

'Even though Alexander Miller disappeared a year after Mr Connolly's death?'

'Mrs Stanton told you the Connolly family had refused to accept Mr Connolly's death was an accident. So we know they had a motive for harming Mr Miller. A year sounds like a long time, but it can take a lot of planning to make someone disappear. Imagine you wanted to make someone disappear, Augusta. How would you go about it?'

She thought for a moment. 'I'm not sure.'

'Exactly. You would need some time to come up with a plan, wouldn't you? And once you had, you might also need some other people to help you. It could take time to convince them. And perhaps Mr Miller was watched for a while. The Connolly family could have observed his movements for some time before taking the opportunity to pounce.'

'Abduct him, you mean?'

'It's a possibility. And if they abducted him, then it was clearly done well because no witnesses came forward.'

Augusta shuddered. 'Abduction, then murder. That's not a nice thought.'

'No, it's not. But if someone intent on revenge spent a year planning it, then they could have done a good job of it.'

'It makes me wonder why the Connolly family wasn't considered at the time.'

'Me too. But from what you've discovered, Augusta, only a cursory search was carried out for Mr Miller. I don't think the police made much effort to delve into his past.'

'If only they had.'

'Indeed. So I think the Connolly family are possible suspects, but there are many other possibilities too.' Philip checked his watch. 'Goodness, I need to get going. Apparently, Charlotte Ramsden has an appointment at a hair salon in Belgravia at half-past ten. I need to loiter around there and keep an eye on her.' He got to his feet.

'Does it seem odd to you?'

'What do you mean?'

'Following a lady around. I know we carried out surveillance during the war. But those people were much more unpleasant than Mrs Ramsden. She's an innocent person.'

'Yes, she is. Her greatest crime appears to be an alleged extra-marital affair. But it's work, Augusta.' He placed his hat on his head. 'I have to get on with what I'm being paid to do.'

Augusta couldn't help wondering if Philip was hoping for a more interesting case to work on as she returned to her shop downstairs. Her thoughts were interrupted by the arrival of a customer.

He was stocky with a square, red face. He removed his hat and headed straight for her without a glance at the books on the shelves.

'Can I help you?' she asked.

'Mrs Peel?'

'Yes.'

'Mr Robert Stanton.' He smiled. But it was a brief smile which didn't reach his eyes. 'I'm the brother-in-law of Alexander Miller,' he said. 'I understand you've spoken to my wife, Jane, on a couple of occasions.'

'That's right.'

His eyes wandered over her figure, and she clenched her fist. She had an aversion to men who made her feel uncomfortable. She positioned herself behind the counter to create a barrier between them.

'What a nice little budgerigar,' he said when his eyes left her and rested on Sparky's cage.

'He's a canary.'

'Is he? What's the difference?'

'They look quite different. It's noticeable in the shape of the beak, head, and tail. Budgerigars are usually larger too.'

'Is that so? I can't say I'm into birds myself. Anyway, I must say I was astonished when I heard all about the letter you found. What a surprise that must have been!' He grinned in an attempt to engage her in the conversation.

'It was a surprise,' she said. 'How can I help you today, Mr Stanton?'

He leant against the counter with his elbow propped on top of it. As if he were chatting to a barmaid at a bar.

'Between you and me, Mrs Peel, my wife suffers terribly with her nerves. I'll speak frankly, if you don't mind? It's quite upset her. She found it difficult not knowing what happened to Alexander. And that's perfectly understandable. But the passage of time has allowed her to live with it as well as she can. All this business with the letter, however, has put us back where we were. She's been terribly upset about it.'

'I'm sorry to hear it, Mr Stanton. It certainly wasn't my intention to upset your wife. I spoke to her because I was interested to find out if she had ever heard anything more from her brother.'

'You were curious, Mrs Peel, and I can understand that. But the involvement of the police has been particularly upsetting to her.'

Augusta thought back to the meeting with Jane Stanton and young Constable Simpson. She had seemed quite comfortable at the time.

'I thought your wife showed little sign of upset when the constable visited,' said Augusta. 'And I asked the police to join us because your wife had previously agreed the letter which supposedly came from her brother was likely to be a forgery. I'm sure you agree, Mr Stanton, that the police need to be involved in that case.'

'Jane hides her emotions well. And she's extremely polite,' he said. 'She would never display any upset or unwillingness to help. But, as her husband, I know her best.'

'She seemed willing to speak to a news reporter,' said Augusta.

'Because of her impeccable politeness, Mrs Peel. She didn't want to turn him away. She would never wish to cause discomfort to other people or hurt their feelings.'

'Even at the expense of her own feelings?'

'Yes. Ridiculous, isn't it? I'm always having words with her about it. Anyway, as a result, she has to nurse her own hurt feelings in private. And that's quite a burden for me to bear, too.'

'Well, please thank your wife for agreeing to speak to me,' said Augusta. 'Even though it was difficult for her.'

He propped himself upright and removed his elbow from the counter. 'I won't be passing that on, Mrs Peel, because she doesn't know I've come to see you. I intend to keep it that way. If she knew I've come here to tell you how upset she was, then she would be mortified. All I can do is urge you to leave her alone now. It's quite apparent no one will ever find out what happened to Alexander, and I sincerely hope you don't give anyone false hope that he may be found again.'

The purpose of Robert Stanton's visit was now clear. He wanted Augusta to stop what she was doing.

'What do you think happened to him, Mr Stanton?' she asked.

'I have no idea. It's an absolute mystery. We were baffled at the time, and we remain baffled ten years on. He was a private man, and his disappearance probably had something to do with someone or something which we knew nothing about.'

'But if a crime has been committed, don't you think justice should be sought?'

'In an ideal world, my answer would be yes, Mrs Peel. But we don't live in an ideal world. Too much time has passed since Alexander's disappearance for anyone to be brought to justice. That's the sad fact of the matter. I trust you'll take my advice and leave the matter alone now, Mrs Peel.'

Fred joined Augusta once Mr Stanton had left.

'I admit I had my ear pressed against the workshop door,' he said. 'So I heard most of that.'

'Good eavesdropping, Fred!' said Augusta. 'We really are turning you into a proper detective.'

'I didn't like the sound of him. I would have joined you at the counter if he'd turned unpleasant.'

'Thank you. He clearly doesn't want me looking into his brother-in-law's disappearance and the obvious question is why.'

'He doesn't seem interested in finding out what happened.'

'No. And that's strange, isn't it? He didn't show any concern for Alexander at all. And his description of his wife being upset doesn't fit with my experience of speaking to her.'

'Perhaps he knows more than he's letting on,' said Fred. 'Perhaps he had something to do with it.'

'After that strange conversation, I think we can consider it a possibility.'

Chapter 17

THE NEWSPAPER REPORTS of Mr Connolly's inquest had included his address in Finchley. Fred had written the address in the notes he had made at the library.

Augusta wondered if the Connolly family still lived at the same address. It would be interesting to travel to Finchley and find out what she could about them. But would she be met with hostility if she asked questions there? After her unpleasant encounter with Mr Stanton, she wasn't keen on the idea of more difficult conversations.

She plucked up the courage that afternoon and asked Fred to mind the shop for her.

'Good luck with the Connollys, Augusta,' he said.

'Thank you, Fred. I think I'll need it.'

The train to Finchley took Augusta through the suburbs of north London. Beyond Hornsey, she caught glimpses of green fields gleaming in the summer sunshine. She also saw the neat rows of new houses encroaching on them. It wouldn't be long before London's northern suburbs reached Finchley.

.   .   .

Arthur Connolly's address had been reported as number 7, College Terrace at the inquest. The street was a short walk from Finchley station. Augusta made her way along a shopping street and turned into a short, narrow street with old cottages on one side. Opposite the cottages was a row of railings, beyond which stood a red-brick Victorian school.

A woman with an eyepatch answered the door. She was about sixty years of age and wore a worn-looking house-coat over her dress.

'Can I help you?' she said, before inhaling on a cigarette.

'Mrs Connolly?' It was a guess and, fortunately for Augusta, it was correct.

'That's right.'

'I hope you don't mind me calling on you. I'm a private detective who's trying to find out what happened to Alexander Miller.'

Mrs Connolly scowled. 'I hope it's not the one I'm thinking of.'

'I'm afraid it is. That's why I called on you.'

'I don't like having his name brought up. I don't like being reminded of what happened to Arthur.'

'I'm very sorry about what happened to Mr Connolly.'

'Why are you sorry? It wasn't your fault. But you ought to be sorry for bringing up Mr Miller's name.'

'Are you aware that he disappeared ten years ago?'

'He disappeared? I took no interest in the man. He should've been locked up for what he did.'

Augusta didn't wish to point out Arthur Connolly's death had been ruled as an accident by a coroner.

'I've been widowed for eleven years now because of him,' added Mrs Connolly. She dropped her cigarette end onto the doorstep and extinguished it with the ball of her foot.

'When did you last see Alexander Miller?'

'When did I last see him? At the inquest. A joke of an inquest, that was. They had the nerve to stand up there and tell everyone Arthur stepped out in front of him. Arthur would never have done such a thing, and I told them that. They said it was the drink. I won't deny Arthur liked his drink, but he could handle himself when he was drunk. He wouldn't have stepped out into the road. I knew him better than anyone and I told the coroner so. I knew it wasn't an accident. Mr Miller was going too fast. It was this road just here.' She stepped out of her door and pointed to her left. 'You can see the hill there, can't you? Miller was racing down that hill. He was going too fast and he never even put his brakes on. My Arthur was at the bottom of the hill, walking home for his tea. And he never got here.' She folded her arms and stared at Augusta with her uncovered eye. 'There's no justice.'

'It must be very difficult for you, even after all these years.'

'It is. And it's even harder when no one was punished for it.' She took a packet of cigarettes from the pocket of her housecoat and offered Augusta one.

'No thank you.'

'So Mr Miller disappeared, did he?' said Mrs Connolly as she lit her cigarette.

'Yes. He vanished about a year after your husband's death.'

'Well, I hope he suffered like we did.'

'I understand your husband's brother visited Mr Miller a week after the inquest.'

'Who told you that?'

'Mr Miller's sister.'

'Oh right. Well, yes. Tom had a word with him. He wanted to tell him what we all thought of him. Because we didn't feel justice had been done.'

'Do you know if Tom threatened him?'

'Tom doesn't mince his words and you don't want to get on the wrong side of him. But that was the last any of us had anything to do with Miller. I told Tom he needn't have done it. There was no need to waste his breath on the man.'

'So no one in your family saw Mr Miller again after your brother-in-law Tom visited him?'

'No. It was left at that.'

'Have you any idea if someone wanted to harm Mr Miller?'

'No. But I'll be honest, Mrs Peel, because I'm the honest type. We all wanted to harm him. I was left a widow because of him and my five children lost their father. The police did nothing about it. But you can't take the law into your own hands. Tom had a word with him and we left it at that. Not a day goes by when I don't think about Arthur. But I'd long forgotten about Miller, so I'm not too happy you brought him up again, Mrs Peel.'

'I apologise. I realise this conversation hasn't been easy for you.'

'Why are you interested in him, anyway?'

'I found a letter from ten years ago in which someone described his disappearance. When I read it, I wondered if he'd been found. But he hasn't, and it's a mystery as to what happened to him.'

'I wouldn't waste your time on him, Mrs Peel. He's not worth thinking about. If I were you, I'd spend my time on something else instead.' She narrowed her eye. 'Where are you from?'

'Bloomsbury.'

'Thought you looked posh.'

'No, I'm not posh. I live above a tailor's shop. And I work in a bookshop.'

'And you're a detective?'

'In my spare time.'

'I've never come across someone like you before. But you seem like a nice young woman.'

'I'm not young.'

Mrs Connolly gave a cackling laugh. 'You're younger than me, so you're young in my eyes. Well, it was nice meeting you, Mrs Peel.' She stepped back into her doorway. 'And take my advice and forget about Miller. He was nothing but trouble.'

Chapter 18

MARY CONNOLLY CLOSED her front door and returned to the kitchen where her son was at the table, finishing his pork chops.

'Who was that?' he asked.

'A woman called Mrs Peel asking about that man, Miller, who hit your dad with his bicycle.'

He sat back and wiped his mouth on his shirtsleeve.

'Why?'

'Miller went missing ten years ago and was never found again.'

'Why did she ask you about him?'

Mary shrugged. 'I don't know. Watch the time, Harry.' She nodded at the clock on the wall. 'You've got to be back at the factory in ten minutes.'

He got to his feet and put on his jacket. 'I want to know why she came round here.' The mention of Miller had agitated him. She knew this by the way he jutted his jaw.

'She told me she found an old letter about Miller's disappearance. She wanted to find out if anyone knew what happened to Mr Miller.'

'I don't see why.'

'Me neither. I never even knew he vanished. I told her I hoped some harm had come to him. I know that's not charitable of me, but it's how I feel after what happened to your father.'

'Maybe he was properly punished for what he did in the end.'

'Mrs Peel knows your Uncle Tom went to see him after the inquest.'

'I wanted to go with him.'

'And I wouldn't let you because I was worried about what you might do. I told you to leave it to Uncle Tom.'

'So does she think Uncle Tom is behind it?'

'I don't know. She thinks Uncle Tom only visited him once. And I told her we left it at that.'

'He saw him more than once.'

'I know. But I didn't tell her that.'

Harry gave a snort. 'And anyway, it's none of her business.'

'That's right. It's not.'

A pause followed and Mary thought about her brother-in-law. Could he have harmed Miller?

'Uncle Tom would never take a life,' said her son, as if reading her thoughts.

'No. He wouldn't.'

'He would hurt someone. And he would hurt him a lot. But he wouldn't take a life.'

'I agree, Harry.'

'He could have scared him off, though.'

'He might have done.'

'Maybe that's what happened.'

'Maybe. But if anyone asks you questions about it, you know nothing about it. Do I make myself clear?'

'Of course. I don't know what Uncle Tom did, so I can't speak for him.'

'Exactly right.' She stepped over to him and patted him on the shoulder. 'You need to get on your way.'

'I don't like it when people come round asking questions.'

'Neither do I, Harry.'

'Mrs Peel must think someone in this family did something to Miller.'

'Well, they didn't. So she shouldn't think that.'

'It makes no difference though, does it, Mum? People always suspect us. Even when we've done nothing wrong.'

She nodded. 'That's true enough.'

'So what if the police get involved?'

'They won't, Harry. It was ten years ago.'

'That didn't stop Mrs Peel calling round, did it? If the police start asking us questions now, then we're for it.'

'We've done nothing wrong, Harry.'

'Even Uncle Tom?'

'I can't speak for him.'

'You need to warn him, Mum.'

'Yes, I suppose I do. He won't like it.'

'Better that he hears it from you than Mrs Peel or the police.'

Mary's stomach gave a turn. 'You're right, Harry.'

Chapter 19

Augusta decided to work on the pile of books in her workshop after her visit to Finchley. She examined the copy of *The Scarlet Pimpernel* which had been left in the box of donated books.

Someone had doodled stick figures on the pages in pencil. Hopefully, the drawings could be removed with a piece of India rubber. The cover was a little faded and in need of a clean. It was otherwise in good condition. Augusta made herself comfortable on a stool at her workbench and began to erase the drawings. She smiled as she carefully rubbed out the little stick people. Someone had clearly entertained themselves on a rainy afternoon by drawing them on the pages. The pencil marks came away quite easily, but she had to work carefully to make sure she didn't damage the page.

Augusta wondered who had drawn the picture and what they had been thinking about at the time. It was going to take a long time to erase all the little stick figures in the book. But she didn't mind. She found the tedium of the work quite calming.

Fred said goodbye to Augusta once he had closed the shop for the day. Augusta worked on and lost track of time. It was eight o'clock when she realised she and Sparky needed to eat.

She was just leaving the shop with Sparky when she saw Philip strolling towards her, leaning on his stick for support.

'You've only just finished, Augusta?'

'I've been repairing some books.'

'Did you finish many?'

'Yes. Three. You've had a long day.'

'Yes, I have.' He sighed. 'Mrs Ramsden traversed the entire length and breadth of London.'

'What was she doing?'

'What wasn't she doing? Actually, I can tell you what she wasn't doing. She wasn't meeting the man she's supposedly having an affair with. There was no sign of him anywhere.'

'Perhaps she hadn't arranged to meet him today.'

'Perhaps not.'

'Are you hungry?'

'No. I've just eaten.'

'Oh.'

'Were you going to suggest something?'

'I'm going home to get something to eat. I was going to invite you to join me if you hadn't eaten yet this evening.'

'Oh, I see. Can I come along anyway?'

'Well, yes. As long as you don't mind watching me have some soup.'

'That was all you were going to offer me? Soup?' Philip smiled.

'I'm afraid so. I'm not much of a cook.'

'Well, even after the meal I've just had, I might be able to manage a little soup.'

As they walked the short distance to Augusta's flat, Philip told her about his day.

'After Mrs Ramsden left the hairdressers in Belgravia, I had to follow her up to Hampstead.'

'By train?'

'No, she took a taxi. So I followed behind in another taxi. She met a friend up there and went for a little walk on the heath.'

'So you had to walk around on Hampstead Heath following them?'

'Yes, I did. Fortunately, it wasn't a very long walk because they then went into Hampstead for some lunch. It was a nice restaurant, actually.'

'You ate there yourself?'

He nodded. 'At a table in the corner.'

'Well, that doesn't sound too difficult.'

'No, it wasn't. I enjoyed that bit. But after that she travelled by taxi back to central London and did some shopping in Covent Garden.'

'You had to follow her around the shops?'

'Yes. That was rather boring. Then she took another long taxi journey down to Richmond. She met a friend in a restaurant there for dinner.'

'And you had to eat in that restaurant too?'

'No, I couldn't see a table suitable for me to hide at. So I had a quick meal at a cheaper restaurant nearby. Not that Richmond has many cheap restaurants. And after I'd dined there, I peered in through the windows of Mrs Ramsden's restaurant periodically.'

'Weren't you worried she would see you?'

'Yes, I'm wary of that. I think some changes to my appearance will help. These are proving quite useful.' He pulled a pair of spectacles out of his pocket and put them on. 'These used to belong to my father.'

Augusta smiled. 'You actually look quite different in them. Do they have proper lenses?'

'Yes. But they're not particularly thick lenses, so I can wear them for a little while before I get a headache.'

Augusta laughed. 'I think you need to buy yourself a pair with clear lenses so they'll be easier to wear.'

'Yes, I think that's an excellent idea, Augusta.'

'Don't tell me you're going to get yourself a false moustache next.'

'The thought has entered my mind. A false moustache can be irritating to wear and there's a risk of it falling off. But if I were to get a small moustache, it hopefully wouldn't cause too much trouble.'

'I was actually joking about the moustache.'

'Oh. I see.'

They reached the door next to the tailor's shop. Augusta unlocked it and they climbed the steps to her flat.

'I'm hoping Mrs Ramsden won't notice me directly,' said Philip. 'But if I can put on a pair of spectacles or change my hat or tie, she might not necessarily recognise me if she sees me more than once. I could try a false beard too.'

'But a false beard might look too strange. And there really is a risk of it falling off. Unless you loop it over your ears and then it would be obviously false. I don't think a beard is a good idea.'

'I'm joking about the beard, Augusta.' He grinned, and they stepped into her flat.

Augusta opened Sparky's cage, and he fluttered up to his favourite spot on the curtain rail.

'Brandy?' said Augusta.

'Yes please.'

They sat in the living area with their drinks. 'I can't deny this surveillance work can be a little boring at times,' said Philip. 'But it's quite straightforward work. I don't think Mrs Ramsden looked in my direction once the entire day. And London is quite an easy place to follow someone around, there's always a crowd to blend into. The taxi journeys were quite expensive, but I can claim my expenses back from Mr Ramsden. He's spending an awful lot of money on this. But then I suppose he's keen to find out if his wife is seeing another man.'

'Judging by the day you had, she isn't.'

'But that was just one day. She was meeting lady friends. So we shall have to see. It will certainly be a bit more exciting if I see her meeting him. At least I'll have something to report back to Mr Ramsden.'

Augusta gave Sparky some pieces of apple. Then she heated up some vegetable soup and placed it on the dining table with slices of fresh bread.

'This soup smells delicious,' said Philip. 'It turns out I really am hungry for something else after all.'

As they ate, Augusta told him about her visit to Mrs Connolly in Finchley. Philip listened with interest.

'Do you think Mrs Connolly was telling you the truth?' he asked.

'Yes, I think she was. She seemed quite genuine to me. I don't think she could have had anything to do with Mr Miller's disappearance. Her brother-in-law, Tom, might know more, though.'

'Because he paid Miller a visit a week after the inquest?'

'Yes. He clearly wanted to have a strong word with him after the inquest found Mr Connolly's death was an accident.'

'I can understand why the Connolly family are upset,' said Philip. 'But from what you've told me about the inquest, it seems the sorry affair really was an accident. I can't imagine Alexander Miller would have deliberately wished to collide with Arthur Connolly. It's not the first time a drunk has stepped out in front of a fast-moving vehicle, and it won't be the last.'

'Your theory that the Connolly family could have planned Mr Miller's disappearance is still a possibility,' said Augusta. 'And I have another suspect in mind, too. Robert Stanton.'

She told Philip about Mr Stanton's visit to her shop that morning.

'He doesn't sound particularly pleasant,' he said.

'He was trying to warn me away, I think.'

'It certainly sounds like it. Do you think Mr Stanton knows something about his brother-in-law's disappearance?'

'I don't know much about him. But from what I saw of him today, I think it's possible. He showed a remarkable lack of concern for Alexander. He didn't seem upset by his disappearance.'

'It was ten years ago. Would he still show upset after all that time?'

'Perhaps not. But there was no sadness or regret, either. Even when someone has died many years previously, people can still talk about them with some sadness or fondness. Just some emotion! But instead, I think Mr Stanton was trying hard to make me like him.'

Philip laughed. 'That ploy clearly didn't work.'

'No it didn't.' Augusta dipped a chunk of bread into her soup.

'It would be good to know a little more about Mr Stanton,' said Philip. 'Perhaps we could discover a motive for him harming his brother-in-law.'

'I think it's interesting that Mr and Mrs Stanton live in his flat. I called at the house they lived in before and it was quite inferior to the Baker Street flat. It's spacious and in a nice location. It's probably worth quite a bit of money.'

'So you could argue that Alexander Miller's sister and husband benefitted from a nice property after he disappeared.'

'Yes. Jane Stanton inherited everything which Alexander left. He wasn't a wealthy man by any means, and she had to apply to a court to have him declared dead.'

'Which is a wait of seven years, isn't it? If the Stantons murdered him for that flat, then it wasn't exactly a quick process to go through.'

'I can't say I warm to Jane Stanton, but I can't imagine her murdering her brother so she could live in his flat.'

'It's rather cold-hearted. But you can't rule it out.'

Chapter 20

LOUISA BRADSHAW CALLED at the bookshop the following day.

'A canary!' she said when she saw Sparky in his cage on the counter. 'I used to have a canary. What's its name?'

'He's called Sparky,' said Augusta.

'I think he's adorable. Does he sing?'

'When he's in the mood.'

Louisa laughed. 'My canary was the same. Very temperamental.' She reached into her bag and pulled out a bundle of papers tied up with string. 'Are you interested in more of my brother's letters?'

'Yes I am!'

Louisa placed the bundle on the counter. 'When I learned Alexander Miller hadn't been found, I wondered if John's other letters held any clues. Mr Miller is mentioned in quite a few of them, but I'm not sure how useful the information is. I'm not a detective like you, Mrs Peel, so I could easily have missed something which might be useful.'

'Thank you Mrs Bradshaw.' Augusta picked up the

bundle. 'I'm sure there's something in these letters which could give us some clues.'

'I have to say John's handwriting was quite dreadful! If you come across any words which are completely illegible, please just ask me about them.'

'I will. This is extremely useful Mrs Bradshaw.'

She sighed. 'All this has got me thinking about John's death again.'

'In what way?'

'I've always accepted his death was an accident. But I'm beginning to wonder about that now. With Alexander still missing, it's clear something unpleasant happened to him. So I wonder the same about John. Perhaps someone pushed him under that train. It's a horrible thought, but I can't help considering it. Perhaps both Alexander and John were murdered.'

'Can you think of anyone who would have wanted to harm John?'

'No. No one at all. But I didn't know everything about his life. There could have been someone he got into trouble with. I just think it's more than a coincidence that something happened to them both in the same year.'

'I agree it needs looking into,' said Augusta. 'The reports from the inquest into your brother's death suggest the witnesses had different opinions about what happened that day.'

'That's true! I remember it at the time. It was strange that the witnesses couldn't completely agree on what they saw. I really didn't know how the coroner was going to make a decision. I must say I'm impressed you've looked into his inquest, Mrs Peel. That's very thorough of you.'

'My assistant, Fred, did most of the work.'

'You have a team of people working for you?'

'No! Fred works here in the shop with me, and he

offered to look up the reporting on the inquest at the library.'

'Well, say thank you to Fred from me.' She checked her watch. 'I need to be on my way. There are a few things I need to do before the children are home from school.'

'Well thank you again, Mrs Bradshaw. I'll let you know if we find something useful in these letters.'

Chapter 21

MARY CONNOLLY FOUND HER BROTHER-IN-LAW, Tom, in the garden of a house he worked at on Dollis Avenue.

'Did you know Alexander Miller went missing?' she said.

He paused from digging a section of the vegetable patch and leant on his shovel. His eyes were screwed up against the bright sunlight and a thin, rolled-up cigarette stuck to his lower lip.

'Miller?' Even at sixty-seven, Tom was leaner and stronger than his younger brother had ever been. He hadn't succumbed to the drink like Arthur had. Mary regretted not having done more to keep her husband away from the pub. Had he turned to drink because she hadn't been good enough for him? Tom had told her she shouldn't blame herself, but she couldn't help it.

'Miller went missing ten years ago,' she said. 'A lady came round yesterday asking me about him.'

'What lady?'

'Mrs Peel. She's a private detective. She's trying to find out what happened to him.'

'Who cares what happened to him?'

'That's what I told her.'

'He probably crashed his bicycle, fell into a ditch and died there. Got eaten by foxes and stray dogs.'

'That's as good an explanation as any, Tom. If she comes asking again, I'll tell her that's probably what happened.'

'It must be. And I'm not sorry about it either. He deserved it. He should have been locked up.'

'That's what I told her. I told her she needn't waste her time finding out what happened to him. The man was no good. He should have been tried for murder.'

'He should have.'

'She knows you paid him a visit.'

Tom's face stiffened, and he pulled the cigarette from his lip. 'She knows about that?'

'She heard it from Miller's sister.'

'Word gets round.' He tossed the cigarette onto the ground and turned it into the earth with his shovel.

'What did you say to him?'

'Oh, you know me, Mary.' He leant on his shovel again. 'I kept it polite.' He grinned, displaying the few teeth he had left.

'How polite?'

'Let's put it this way. It wasn't difficult to frighten him. He was a bit of a weakling.'

'You threatened him?'

'I can't remember everything I said, Mary. It was years ago.'

'Was he scared?'

'Let's just say he was probably watching his back for a few weeks after.'

'You visited him again, didn't you?'

He took off his cap, scratched his head, then replaced

it again. 'A few times. I just thought he needed reminding. You know how it is. He was walking about a free man while my brother was in his grave. It wasn't right.'

'No, it wasn't.' A robin landed on a low wall. They watched it as it cocked its head, appearing to survey the freshly dug earth.

Tom smiled. 'There he is again, the little fellow. Looking for more worms. Must have some babies to feed.'

'Maybe Miller's still alive somewhere.'

'Like where?'

She shrugged. 'I don't know.'

'No, he can't be. He wasn't the sort to take himself off somewhere. His life was too comfortable for that. Had a good job working for the railways. Not *on* the railways, mind. He had a much easier job than that, working in an office. He had a nice flat too. He probably fell into a ditch, like I said.'

'With all these people suddenly wondering what happened to him, they might ask us questions.'

'Why?'

'Because they might think we had something to do with it.'

'We didn't.'

'But people don't see it like that, do they? They know what sort of people we are and we're easy to blame.'

'No one can blame me for something I haven't done.'

'But you know what the police are like. They might think we took revenge on Miller.'

'I can't see them doing anything about it ten years later.'

'But they might, Tom.'

'Stop worrying about it, Mary.' He seized his shovel and thrust it into the ground. The muscles in his forearms rippled as he turned the earth over. She could tell the conversation was angering him. And she knew better than to be on the receiving end of his temper.

'What shall I say if someone asks me questions again?' she said.

He paused. His eyes were narrow and dark now.

'You don't know anything, Mary. That's what you tell them.'

Chapter 22

AFTER CLOSING the shop that evening, Augusta walked back to her flat with Sparky in his cage and the bundle of John Gibson's letters in her bag. She was looking forward to reading them and hopefully finding some more clues about Alexander Miller's disappearance.

She was by the newsagent's shop on Marchmont Street when she heard the voice behind her.

'Mrs Peel!'

The hairs on the back of her neck prickled. It was a voice she didn't like.

She turned to see a man in a dull, grey suit. He had a neat red moustache and his wide-set eyes rested on her coldly.

It was Walter Ferguson from the *London Weekly Chronicle*. The reporter who had claimed to have discovered her real name.

'What do you want?' she said.

'I was wondering if you received my letter, Mrs Peel.'

'I did. Were you expecting a reply?'

'I thought there would be some sort of response.'

The man seemed rather desperate for her attention. She imagined he led quite a lonely existence.

'I didn't respond because I didn't feel the need to.'

'But surely you're going to be rather upset when I tell people your real name?'

'Do you want me to be upset?'

'I'm just interested in finding out what your reaction will be.'

'Haven't you got better things to be doing, Mr Ferguson?'

'I've got lots of things to be getting on with. But I can't help being fascinated by your story, Mrs Peel. A middle-aged lady who runs a bookshop in Bloomsbury has a secret past as an intelligence officer. It's very compelling indeed. It's the sort of story you would find in a book or a play. I suppose I can't help being captivated by it. And the fact you have lied about your identity...'

'I haven't lied. Most of the people who worked in intelligence during the war had to take on a new identity.'

'But you kept yours, Mrs Peel. Mr Fisher didn't, did he? He went back to the name he'd used before.'

She took a step towards him. 'Where are you getting this information from, Mr Ferguson? Have you asked someone at the War Office to look at confidential files? Because if you have, I suspect both you and your informer are breaking the law.'

'Are you trying to threaten me, Mrs Peel?'

'No. But you'll be in trouble if you're doing something illegal.'

'What have you got to hide, Mrs Peel?'

She felt her jaw clench. 'My history is my business. If someone I trust were to ask me about my past, then I would answer them truthfully. But I don't have to explain myself to you. I have done nothing malicious or deceitful. I should be allowed to go about my daily life without harassment from people like you.'

'But what about the people _you_ harass, Mrs Peel? Don't you think they deserve to be left alone too?'

'I'm not harassing anyone, Mr Ferguson, nor have I ever done. I ask people questions when I'm investigating a case, but I'm respectful about it. Particularly when someone is uncomfortable about discussing the topic. It's not harassment. However, illegally obtaining information about someone's past and publishing it in a newspaper is harassment. As is loitering on the street and waiting for them to turn up.'

'How do you know I've been loitering here, Mrs Peel? I could have just been passing through.'

'I doubt it. You know I live here. What do you actually want from me?'

'I don't want anything from you, Mrs Peel. But I think people deserve to know the truth about you.'

'Which people?'

'The people who trust you. They don't know who you really are.'

'I don't understand why that's of any interest to you.'

'I'm a news reporter. A journalist. It's my job to uncover the truth.'

'If it's in the public interest, perhaps. But if it's just a vendetta against someone, then it's not your job at all.'

'A vendetta?' He laughed. 'I'm not the sort of person who pursues vendettas.'

'I disagree, Mr Ferguson. I asked you some questions about your former colleague who was tragically murdered. And from that moment on, you embarked on this strange campaign to supposedly tell people the truth about me. I don't know what you're hoping to achieve.'

'Justice, Mrs Peel.'

'I think you have a warped idea of what justice is.'

He laughed again. 'By the way, I must congratulate you on finding the letter which received such enthusiastic coverage in the *Daily London News*.'

'The newspaper coverage was not something I planned.'

'No, I don't expect it was. You're the modest type, aren't you, Mrs Peel? At least that's what you'd like people to think.'

Her heart pounded but she tried to remain calm. 'Well, I can't stand about here chatting with you all evening, Mr Ferguson. Much as I'd like to.' She forced a wide smile and went on her way.

'Keep an eye out for a new article about you, Mrs Peel,' he called after her.

She ignored him and her heart pounded harder. Was he really going to publish her real name?

Chapter 23

AUGUSTA TRIED to push Walter Ferguson out of her mind as she sat down at her dining table to read John Gibson's letters. She arranged them on the table in date order and decided to read them chronologically. There were thirty-six letters in all. Most of them were long and the handwriting was difficult to decipher. It was obvious that reading them all would not be a quick, easy job.

Sparky fluttered about the room, and Augusta sipped her soup as she read about John Gibson and Alexander Miller's cycling excursions to various places on the outskirts of London. John wrote well and his descriptions of some places were so compelling that Augusta felt persuaded to visit them herself. She enjoyed his descriptions of the deer in Richmond Park, the quaintness of Harrow on the Hill, and the grandeur of Hampton Court Palace and its grounds. John mentioned Alexander's ability to cycle faster than him up hills. Alexander put it down to his daily intake of Jackson's Blood Purifier and suggested John take it too.

The effort of deciphering the handwriting in dim, artificial light made Augusta's eyes sore after a while. She had thought in recent months that she probably needed reading glasses.

She had a break from reading the letters and made herself some cocoa.

'Well I haven't learnt much more about Alexander Miller yet,' she said to Sparky. He watched her from the top of the clock in the kitchen. 'But I've only read four letters so far. Perhaps I can manage one more before bedtime.'

Augusta returned to her dining table with her mug of cocoa and picked up the next letter in the sequence. After deciphering the first few sentences, she realised this letter was a little more interesting than the previous ones.

I have behaved quite deplorably and I feel ashamed of it now. It was while Alexander and I were cycling to Teddington. He mentioned Jemima Kemp and, in doing so, quite upset me.

Jemima is a young lady who works as a secretary in our offices. She is quite pretty. You know I'm shy when it comes to the fairer sex, Louisa, so I've only spoken to her a few times. Although she is friendly, I can feel myself blushing when I speak to her. My bashfulness is irritating. I wish I could be more confident when speaking to Jemima.

For some time now, I have had a desire to see more of her. But I feel much too shy to ask her if she would like to meet outside work. And I'm afraid she'll turn me down. So I have admired Jemima from afar for some time.

Imagine my shock when Alexander told me how fond he was of her! And he asked me if I thought it was a good idea if he asked her to go to the pictures with him. Can you imagine how I felt? Alexander is a good friend of mine, but I found it quite difficult to hide my envy when he mentioned this. I feel sure I've admired Jemima for longer than him and his mention of her made me realise I should muster up the courage to ask her out myself. If only I had done it. Then Alexander wouldn't have got the same idea!

So I'm ashamed to admit I told Alexander a lie. I told him I had seen her with a boyfriend and she had been going steady with him for a while. Alexander was surprised and very disappointed. He had never seen the boyfriend, and that's because the boyfriend doesn't exist. Not to my knowledge, anyway. The man I told him about was entirely fictional. But I said it because I didn't want Alexander to ask Jemima out for the evening. It was selfish of me. Especially as I think she would prefer him over me, anyway. He has more confidence, and he's certainly more handsome.

And now I find myself in a troublesome spot. How can I ask Jemima out for myself after I've told Alexander she has a boyfriend? I would have to invent a story about their relationship ending. And surely if I asked her out, then Alexander would realise that I had made up the story. So I've dug myself into a bit of a hole, and I only have myself to blame. It's quite ridiculous. It's torment when a woman drives a wedge between two friends. And poor Jemima is oblivious to all of it!

Chapter 24

AUGUSTA TOLD Fred about Jemima the following morning.

'Oh dear,' he said. 'Alexander and John both fell for the same woman?'

'It seems so. I've still got a lot of letters to read so I don't know what the full story is yet. But learning about Jemima has given me a new thought. Perhaps the answer to Alexander's disappearance has something to do with the affection they both had for Jemima. Maybe John was behind Alexander's disappearance.'

'You think John murdered his friend?' said Fred.

'It's a possibility, isn't it? From what I've learned about John Gibson, it seems he was a pleasant young man. But when he discovered his friend also liked Jemima, he lied to him and told him she was courting someone. He clearly felt bad about lying to Alexander because he confessed to his sister what he'd done. But maybe his envy got the better of him?'

'It could have done,' said Fred.

Movement outside the window caught Augusta's eye. A man of about sixty was peering in at the shop. He wore a flat cap and a thin cigarette drooped from his mouth. When he caught Augusta's eye, he moved on.

She turned back to Fred. 'In his letter, John describes Alexander as being more confident and handsome than him,' she said. 'Maybe he was unsure he would ever win Jemima's affection but was also keen to prevent someone else from being with her.'

'Even his own friend.'

'Yes. Quite selfish, really.'

'And yet quite common,' said Fred. 'It is a situation which can lead to murder.'

'And John's death later that year could be for two reasons,' said Augusta. 'Either someone knew he was behind Alexander's disappearance and took their revenge. Or he felt so awful about what he'd done that he deliberately jumped in front of the train.'

'But if someone had known John was behind Alexander's disappearance, surely they would have reported it to the police,' said Fred. 'I think it's unlikely they would have taken matters into their own hands and pushed him under a train. I think the second explanation is more likely. John was so consumed by guilt about what he did to Alexander that he jumped in front of the train. That's not unheard of, is it? Someone commits murder and they can't live with themselves afterwards.'

'So perhaps John Gibson is our only suspect,' said Augusta. 'It's going to be difficult to establish where he was at the time of Alexander's disappearance.'

'But let's not forget John did a lot of work to try to find out what had happened to Alexander. Would he have done that if he was guilty?'

'Yes, because he would have been keen to act as normally as possible. Perhaps he wished to show how concerned he was about his friend so that no one would suspect him?'

'And it seems no one did.'

'Exactly. So his plan worked.'

There was a pause as they considered this idea. Fred scratched his chin as he thought. 'This could be the answer, Augusta. But if it's not, then I feel quite guilty accusing John Gibson of murder.'

'We have to consider everyone,' said Augusta. 'And I'm not sure why I didn't think of him sooner. We need to find out what happened about Jemima. Did she choose Alexander over John? There may be some clues in John's letters. But his sister, Mrs Bradshaw, must know more. I'm going to pay her a visit.'

They heard footsteps on the staircase and a smartly dressed, tall man with grey hair came into view.

'Hello again, Mr Ramsden,' said Augusta.

'Hello!' He reached the bottom of the stairs. 'I've just had a meeting with your colleague, Mr Fisher, and I thought I'd come down here and purchase a few more books from you.'

'Have you already read the ones you bought last time?'

'Oh yes. I'm a voracious reader, I'm afraid! I would probably save a bit of money by borrowing from the library. But I often forget to return books and run up large fines. So it suits me to buy books instead. And one can justify the cost when it comes to second-hand books. Your books are well-priced, Mrs Peel, and they're almost all as good as new!'

Mr Ramsden was in a jovial mood, which suggested Philip hadn't yet found any evidence of his wife's affair.

'I can look after Mr Ramsden if you need to get on your way, Augusta,' said Fred.

Augusta thanked him. 'Hopefully we'll find out more about Jemima.'

~

Louisa Bradshaw's housekeeper answered the door of her Notting Hill home. Augusta sensed something was wrong when the housekeeper planted herself firmly in the doorway.

'Mrs Bradshaw is not receiving visitors at the present time.' Her gaze was steely.

'Oh dear. Has something happened?'

'I am following her instructions, madam.'

'But Mrs Bradshaw is alright?'

'She wishes to be left in peace.'

'I see. Well, would you pass on my best wishes to her? I hope she's alright and I hope to speak with her again soon. I have a few more questions about her brother.'

'Mrs Bradshaw wishes to be left in peace, so I shall not be bothering her with messages. I wish you a good day, Mrs Peel.'

Augusta felt her jaw drop as the door was closed on her. She took a few steps back and looked up at the house. The only sound in the street was the cheerful song of birds in the trees.

As Augusta turned to go, she caught a movement in the corner of her eye. Someone at a window, perhaps?

She surveyed the house again but saw no sign of anyone.

Augusta went on her way.

It would have been easy to feel offended by her reception at Louisa Bradshaw's home.

But Augusta felt worried. What had happened to her?

Chapter 25

LOUISA BRADSHAW STOOD BACK from the window as she watched Mrs Peel walk away.

'I told her you weren't receiving visitors,' came her housekeeper's voice from behind her. 'That's what you wanted me to say, wasn't it, Mrs Bradshaw?'

'Yes. That's right. Thank you, Mrs Wilson. What did she say?'

'She passed on her best wishes. She seemed concerned about you.'

'Did she?' Louisa continued to gaze out of the window, twisting her handkerchief in her hands. She liked Mrs Peel. She hoped she wasn't offended that she had refused to see her.

She wished she could explain to Mrs Peel that she had been warned not to speak to her.

It was too dangerous.

'I shall get on with preparing the vegetables for dinner.'

'Thank you, Mrs Wilson.'

Chapter 26

'TEA! What a lovely thought. Thank you, Augusta!' said Philip when she placed the cup on his desk.

'I only bring you tea when I need your help with something,' she said as she sat in the chair across the desk from him.

'I've noticed that. Have you found out anything more about Alexander Miller?'

Augusta told him about John Gibson's letters and the hostile reception she had received at Louisa Bradshaw's house that morning.

'I wonder why she isn't talking to anyone,' said Philip.

'I don't know if she's refusing to speak to everyone, or just refusing to speak to me.'

'Why would it be just you?'

'Maybe because she finds it upsetting talking about her brother.'

'In which case, the housekeeper could have politely explained that to you.'

'I suppose so. I just hope Louisa Bradshaw is alright.'

'There's not much you can do about it, Augusta.

Clearly something has happened to her, and she doesn't wish to discuss it with anyone.'

'I'd hoped she'd be able to tell me more about Jemima.'

'It's a shame you haven't been able to speak to her again. Hopefully, you'll find more in those letters you're painstakingly deciphering.'

'It certainly takes a while and a lot of patience. I can't help wondering what happened. Did John and Alexander fall out over Jemima? Did John get rid of Alexander?'

'It's possible.'

'I could enquire at the accounts department at the Great Western Railway headquarters. All three of them worked there.'

'That's an excellent idea, Augusta. I'm sure you'll find someone there who'll be able to tell you a little more about the three of them.'

Augusta took a sip of tea. 'Mr Ramsden seems jolly. He bought four more books from me this morning.'

Philip smiled. 'I'm pleased he's good for your business, Augusta.'

'Thank you for sending him my way. You don't have to follow Mrs Ramsden about today?'

'No. Apparently she has a head cold, so she's spending a few days at home. She'll soon be over it, no doubt, with the help of treatments from Mr Ramsden's company, Hodgson Medicines. In fact, he's donated a few medicines to me.' Philip opened his desk drawer and took out some small brown bottles. 'I've got Camrol Compound for coughs and colds, Lorine Lozenges to soothe the throat, and Perratin Pills for dyspepsia.' He lined them up on his desk. 'Are you in need of any of these, Augusta?'

'No, I'm perfectly fit and well at the moment, Philip. But it's reassuring to know you have the contents of a medicine cabinet in your drawer.'

'It is, isn't it?' He put the bottles away again. 'I call it peace of mind. By the way, you haven't commented on my blackboard yet.'

It was propped up on an easel in the corner of the room.

'I didn't notice it!' said Augusta. 'What are you going to write on it?'

'Notes about the cases I'm working on. I don't have many of them at the moment, but it will come in useful when I have.'

'It will.' Augusta drained her tea. 'I haven't told you yet why I need some help. I had an encounter with Walter Ferguson.'

'Ferguson?' Philip scowled. His good mood had completely evaporated by the time Augusta had finished telling him about the conversation.

'The man has a nerve!' he said. 'He was clearly waiting for you on Marchmont Street, wasn't he? He knows you live there. What a rat! I should ask someone to arrest him just for the sake of it.'

'There's no need. I didn't feel like I was in danger. He's just a nuisance.'

'And he says he's going to publish another article about you?'

'Yes, apparently he is.'

'I said I was going to speak to the editor of the *London Weekly Chronicle*, didn't I? And then I've been so busy following Mrs Ramsden about that it slipped my mind. I shall do it immediately, Augusta. They can't be allowed to print confidential information from government files.'

'There's a possibility Ferguson hasn't found out anything about me and is merely hoping I'll be intimidated by the threat.'

'He shouldn't be intimidating you, Augusta! I wish you would agree to me getting him arrested for something.'

'Arresting him would only help his cause,' said Augusta. 'He wants attention more than anything else. That's why he sought me out to find out what I thought about his letter. He couldn't bear the fact I hadn't acknowledged it. If you could speak to the editor, I would be very grateful. But I think we should try to achieve it while giving Ferguson as little attention as possible.'

Chapter 27

'A PRIVATE DETECTIVE?' said Mr Shaw. 'There are quite a few of you about. Especially lady ones. It seems to be a trend these days.'

He gestured for Augusta to sit in the chair at his desk. Mr Shaw had wisps of thin white hair and a thin white moustache. He was a senior accounts officer in the accounts department at the headquarters of the Great Western Railway. The window of his office overlooked the soot-stained glass and iron arches of Paddington railway station.

'Lady detectives are a trend?' said Augusta, as she sat.

'Oh yes. Twenty years ago, they weren't around at all. But these days they seem to be everywhere. It must have been the war. It changed everything, didn't it?'

'Yes, it did.'

'Now then…' He put on some wiry reading glasses and examined a piece of paper in front of him. 'My secretary says you wish to speak to me about Alexander Miller and John Gibson.'

'That's right.'

He whipped the reading glasses off again.

'I can confirm they both worked here. It was some time ago now and I'm probably one of the few people here who still remembers them. So you're lucky you're speaking with me!' He grinned.

'Lucky?'

'Indeed. And Mr Miller and Mr Gibson are both sadly missed.'

'Mr Miller disappeared ten years ago.'

'Very sad indeed.'

'Do you have any idea what could have happened to him?'

'No idea at all. Mr Gibson told me that a letter had been sent to Mr Miller's sister informing her he'd moved to another part of the country. That seemed odd to me. There was no indication he'd planned to do such a thing. And if he had planned it, then he would have been a responsible chap and given four weeks' notice to terminate his employment with us. I can't see why he would have walked out on his job like that. He enjoyed his work here, and he was good at what he did. His sudden disappearance was alarming.'

'His sister believes the letter was forged.'

'I didn't know Mr Miller as well as his sister did, so it's not my place to decide whether or not he wrote it. But it seemed out of character. And if Mr Miller's sister suspects he didn't write the letter, then I can believe he didn't.'

'John Gibson seemed to do all he could to find his friend.'

'Yes, he did. He was extremely upset about Mr Miller's sudden disappearance. As we all were. Mr Gibson didn't believe Alexander would have deliberately gone off. He took it rather badly and I think that's why the accident came about at Baker Street station. I think he'd had enough.'

'You think Mr Gibson fell under the train deliberately?'

'It's awful to say it, I know. But he really was quite upset about his friend's disappearance.'

'Do you think someone could have pushed Mr Gibson?'

'If they had, then I'm sure something would have come out about it. Someone would have seen something. Having seen how much Mr Miller's disappearance upset him, I'm afraid I think the accident resulted from deliberate action on his part. Very upsetting, I know.'

'Do you remember a lady called Jemima who worked as a secretary in this department when Mr Miller and Mr Gibson were working here?'

A smile spread across his face. 'Jemima Kemp. She was a treasure!'

It was clear she had left an impression on Mr Shaw as well as Miller and Gibson.

'She worked here for a couple of years before she got married. A pretty girl she was.' His gaze drifted off into the middle-distance. 'She was what I'd describe as a proper English rose.'

Augusta felt a snap of impatience. 'Did she have a relationship with Mr Miller or Mr Gibson?'

'You're asking the wrong man, I'm afraid, Mrs Peel. I was too old to know about the affairs of the young people here. Even back then.'

'Do you know where she is now?'

'When she married, she and her new husband moved out to the suburbs. Wimbledon rings a bell.'

'Do you know her married name?'

'Campbell, I believe. Her husband is Jeffrey Campbell,

a Scottish doctor. I wonder what Jemima looks like now? Quite different, I should imagine.'

'Thank you. I shall speak to her next.'

'Oh, I shouldn't think she'd be able to tell you much. She worked in the same office as the two gentlemen and that was about it.'

'From what I understand, both Mr Miller and Mr Gibson were quite fond of her.'

'Well, they would have been! Everyone was fond of Jemima.' He chuckled. 'I was too. And I was approaching sixty and had been happily married for thirty-seven years!'

He had presumably been expecting Augusta to laugh with him, because his smile quickly disappeared when he realised she wasn't.

'Thank you very much for your time, Mr Shaw.' She got to her feet.

'It's been a pleasure, Mrs Peel. I'm not sure what you're trying to find out, but good luck with it anyway. And if you do speak to Mrs Jemima Campbell, please pass on my regards.'

Chapter 28

AUGUSTA SAT down to read more of John Gibson's letters that evening. Frustratingly, the next few didn't mention Jemima. Instead, they described more cycling excursions and a complaint that Jackson's Blood Purifier had done nothing to improve John's cycling uphill. He seemed irritated that Alexander could cycle faster than him.

'Jemima Campbell,' said Augusta, sitting back in her chair. Sparky eyed her from the top of the shade on the table lamp. 'She should be fairly easy to find in Wimbledon, shouldn't she, Sparky? Perhaps Fred could help me find her address by looking in the directory. He's becoming quite useful in this investigation.'

She wondered for a moment if any other detectives discussed cases with their canaries, then picked up the next letter. Her eyes strained as she tried to decipher the words. Then a sentence aroused her interest: "Alexander was in a dreadfully bad mood as we cycled to Epsom." Augusta read on, keen to find out why.

'How interesting,' she said to Sparky once she reached

the end of the letter. 'It seems Alexander lent his sister, Jane Stanton, some money. And he got rather fed up when she failed to repay him.'

Chapter 29

Augusta made her way to Baker Street the following morning. It was warm and sunny, so she decided to walk. Her forty-minute route took her through the bustling streets of Bloomsbury, Fitzrovia and Marylebone. She passed elegant old townhouses, towering red-brick apartment buildings and lively shops and cafes. Barrels of beer were being unloaded outside public houses and newspaper sellers shouted out the day's headlines.

As she walked, Augusta considered Robert Stanton's recent visit. He had advised her to stop looking into Alexander Miller's disappearance. A mild threat. Was it because he was worried she would discover the family conflict over money?

His lack of concern for his missing brother-in-law made more sense to her now. From what Augusta had read in the most recent letter, it was possible Alexander Miller and his sister had not been on good terms at the time of his death.

She hoped Robert Stanton was currently at work and that she would find Jane Stanton alone.

Her apprehension grew as she reached the hairdresser's shop below the Stanton's flat. If Mr Stanton was at home, then he was likely to be angered by her visit. Augusta decided it was a risk she would have to take. She was keen to find out how Jane Stanton was going to explain the money she had borrowed from her brother.

Augusta was relieved when Mrs Stanton answered the door. But the coolness in her expression suggested she wasn't happy to see Augusta there.

'I've said all I need to say,' said Mrs Stanton. 'I really have nothing else to add.'

'Have you heard from the police about the forged letter yet?'

'No. And I don't really expect to. There's nothing more they can do.'

She moved to close the door and Augusta realised she only had a few seconds left in which to grab her attention. 'Did you ever pay back the money which you owed your brother?' she hurriedly asked.

Mrs Stanton froze. 'I beg your pardon?'

'I'm reading some letters which John Gibson wrote. He describes your brother being angry about some money you owed him.'

Her expression hardened. 'Why on earth was Alexander discussing money with a friend he went cycling with?'

'I can't answer that, Mrs Stanton. It's just something which was written in the letter.'

'He had no business discussing that!' She sneered at Augusta, as if she were responsible for it.

'You can tell me your side of the story, Mrs Stanton. I'm not passing judgment on you.'

'I'm sure you are. You'd probably be delighted to

uncover some ugly business between me and Alexander. No family is perfect, you know.'

'I'm aware of that.'

Jane Stanton folded her arms. 'You're prying too much, Mrs Peel. Robert warned me about you, and I thought he was making a fuss. But I can see what he meant by it now. Where are these letters? I want to see them!'

Augusta chose her words carefully. 'They're the property of John Gibson's sister.'

'Then I shall call on her and kindly request that she destroys them.'

'May I ask why?'

'Because there's no use in revisiting these events again.'

'There is if we can find out what happened to your brother. Aren't you the least bit interested?'

'Of course I'm interested! But I also know it's a waste of time. You won't find anything out. I've told you this already. And all you're succeeding in doing is airing my family's dirty laundry.'

'You're the first person I've discussed this with,' said Augusta. She was tempted to add she had also discussed it with her canary but thought better of it. 'Did you owe your brother money at the time of his disappearance, Mrs Stanton?'

'I don't have to answer that.'

Augusta reasoned that if she had repaid the money, she would have admitted it.

'Alright then. Thank you for your time.' She turned to leave and made her way to the staircase.

'I want those letters!' Mrs Stanton called after her.

'Then I suggest you speak to Mrs Bradshaw about them.'

Chapter 30

'THERE ARE letters about the money you owed Alexander?' said Robert Stanton as he poured himself a large whisky.

'Yes, apparently so.' His wife sat on the sofa, her hands fidgeting in her lap. 'Alexander moaned to his friend that I wasn't paying him back.'

Typical of Alexander, Robert thought. *He could never be relied on to keep his mouth shut.* He took a large gulp of his drink and enjoyed the burn at the back of his throat. Then he topped up his glass and positioned himself in the centre of the room, facing Jane.

'We need to get hold of those letters,' she said.

'Who's got them?'

'Alexander's friend's sister.'

'Then get them from her tomorrow.'

'But what if she doesn't give them to me?'

'Then I'll have a word with her.'

'In what way?'

'Never mind. Just call on her tomorrow and ask for them. See where it gets you. What else is in the letters?'

'I don't know.' She bit her lip and her eyes darted

around the room. He knew she felt ashamed about the debt. She was horrified someone else had learned about it.

'I didn't think Alexander would discuss that sort of thing with someone else!' she said. 'What else did he tell him?'

'I don't know. He was your brother.'

'But I borrowed that money for...' She bit her lip again as she trailed off. He knew what she wanted to say. But was she brave enough?

'I borrowed that money for both of us,' she said. 'It wasn't just for me, was it?'

'And what does that have to do with anything?' He stared down at her.

'The money was for both you and me. We both borrowed it, didn't we?'

'What are you trying to say, Jane?'

He knew she was trying to say she had borrowed the money for him. Despite his employment at the bank, his salary had never been quite enough for them.

'You were the one who asked Alexander for the money,' he said. 'Not me.' He drained his drink.

'But you...'

'What? Asked you to?'

Jane pursed her lips and gave a nod.

'I don't remember what I did.' He marched back to the whisky decanter. 'It was over ten years ago, Jane.'

Robert's jaw clenched as he thought about Augusta Peel. Why had she ignored his request to stay away? Had he not made himself clear enough?

'I gave that money to you, Robert,' said Jane.

He turned to see she had got up from her seat. He stepped towards her, and she backed away.

'We both needed the money,' he said. 'You said that just a minute ago.'

'Yes, but—'

He interrupted her. 'I don't want to hear any more.' He pointed at the sofa, and she sat down again. 'You brought this on yourself, Jane. You spoke to that woman, Mrs Peel, when she called round here. And then you spoke to the press! If you're worried people have found out things about you, then you only have yourself to blame.'

'I didn't—'

'Don't argue with me!'

Silence fell. He took another gulp from his glass. What could he do about Mrs Peel? The woman was a nuisance.

Jane gave a sniff, then spoke in a timorous voice. 'I just wish we had paid the money back to Alexander.'

'Why? Everything he had became yours in the end, didn't it? It wouldn't have made the slightest difference. Sometimes you really do talk nonsense, Jane.'

'What if Mrs Peel mentions the money to the police? It doesn't look good that we owed my brother money when he vanished.'

'*You* owed him money, Jane. Not me.'

'But—'

'What did I say?' He raised a warning finger, and she was quiet again. 'Just get those letters back, Jane. And get them destroyed.'

Chapter 31

'Jane Stanton owed Alexander Miller money?' said Philip as he stood in Augusta's workshop that evening. She had been busy mending a copy of *The Enchanted Castle* when he had knocked at her workshop door. 'How much money?'

'I don't know. I didn't ask Mrs Stanton because she didn't want to discuss it with me. Maybe I'll find out from the letters.'

Philip rested against the workshop table. 'And Mrs Stanton didn't repay him?'

'She wouldn't say. But I think she would have told me if she had.'

'Yes, I think she would have done too. This is interesting. It could be a motive for Mr and Mrs Stanton harming Miller. They borrowed money from him and couldn't pay it back. Perhaps he was harassing them for it and they decided to get rid of him.'

'And then benefit from inheriting his estate seven years later,' said Augusta.

'I wonder what they were doing at the time of Miller's

disappearance? It's almost impossible to establish alibis for people a decade later.'

'It might be worth a try,' said Augusta.

Philip gave a laugh. 'I don't think I'd be able to persuade the police to do anything on it, though. They're busy enough as it is. We need more evidence first.'

'Such as what?'

'I don't know. This is a tricky case. And I don't have many good ideas at the moment. Today has been an unproductive day.'

'Oh dear. Why?'

'I called at the offices of the *London Weekly Chronicle* to speak to the editor about Ferguson's article. But he was out. And then, Charlotte Ramsden noticed me while I was watching her.'

'How?'

'It couldn't really be helped. We were in the Lyons Corner House in Piccadilly and a thief tried to steal her handbag. She'd rested it on the seat next to her as she sat with a friend. He marched past, grabbed it, and ran off.'

'Oh no!'

'He headed for the door and his route happened to take him past the table I was sitting at. I had to do something. So I lunged sideways and rugby-tackled him.'

'You got her handbag back?'

'I did. Some customers sat on him once he was on the floor and he couldn't get away. He had to stay there until the police arrived.'

'You're a hero, Philip!'

His face reddened. 'I don't know about that. I just did what anyone else would have done in that situation.'

'I don't think many people would be brave enough to rugby-tackle a thief. Did you hurt yourself?'

'Not really. I came off my chair and ended up on the floor with him. My bad leg's a little sore, but I'm fine.'

'Mrs Ramsden must have been very grateful.'

'That's the trouble. She was. She sat with me at my table for a while afterwards. She asked me my name and I told her I was Albert Clark. She's a friendly, chatty lady.'

'How friendly?'

'Really quite friendly. I don't want to cast aspersions on the lady's character, she's perfectly respectable and pleasant. However, she had a way about her which...'

'Which what?'

'She has a rather endearing way about her. She fluttered her eyelashes at me.'

'Oh, I see. She's one of those ladies.'

'I don't mean it like that, Augusta. As I've said, I don't want to cast aspersions on her character. But perhaps I can understand why Mr Ramsden has some concerns about her seeing another gentleman.'

Augusta smiled. 'So she made eyes at you?'

'I wouldn't describe it as that.' His face reddened some more. 'But I'm a little younger than her. About twenty years younger, in fact. And I think she was instantly rather fond of me because I came to her rescue.'

'It's not surprising, I suppose. And you no doubt charmed her.'

'I didn't charm her!'

'But she must have found you charming.'

'Possibly. I don't know. Anyway, I was there for a while as she chatted to me, and I had to make excuses to extricate myself in the end.'

'She seems to have recovered quite quickly from her head cold,' said Augusta. 'Maybe it was her husband's Camrol Compound which did it. Do you think she suspects you've been following her?'

'No, I don't think so at all. But now that she's spoken to me, I can't conduct the surveillance effectively, can I? She may spot me again and recognise me. I've been careless.'

'You haven't been careless, Philip. You intervened to stop a thief from stealing her handbag.'

'I did it without thinking, really. It all happened so quickly. I couldn't bear the thought of him getting away with it.'

'Are you going to tell Mr Ramsden that she spoke to you?'

'I'll have to. I may have to stop doing this work for him. I'm supposed to be following her about incognito. It's no good if she knows who I am.'

'You could put on one of your disguises.'

'I could. But I don't think spectacles and an itchy moustache would be enough.'

Augusta smiled. 'Your trouble is that you're too nice, Philip.'

'Too nice? I don't think so. I just try to be a normal person, Augusta. I don't like the thought of being rude and unhelpful. Although if I had been, then I probably wouldn't be in this predicament now.'

Chapter 32

'VEGETABLE SOUP AGAIN?' said Anthony Ramsden as the maid spooned it into his bowl. 'Didn't we have vegetable soup last night?'

'It was the night before,' said his wife, Charlotte. 'We had tomato soup last night. Isn't that right, Milly?'

'Yes, that's right, Mrs Ramsden.'

'Vegetable soup for the second time this week, then,' said Anthony as he tucked his serviette into his collar.

'Yes, but it's very good soup,' said Charlotte. 'There's no need to be grumpy about it.'

They ate in silence for a minute and Anthony grudgingly acknowledged to himself the soup was good.

'The most unusual thing happened today,' said Charlotte. 'A knight in shining armour came to my aid.'

'A knight in shining armour? You were a damsel in distress, were you?'

'Yes, I was. I made the mistake of going to the Lyons Corner House in Piccadilly.'

'Good grief, Charlotte. Why on earth did you go there?'

'Annie and I hadn't planned to. But we were tired from shopping, and it was the nearest place. And besides, say what you like about Lyons Corner Houses, but they do a perfectly decent cup of tea there. So there we were, having a chat about Annie's daughter's wedding, when a young man snatched my handbag!'

'Goodness. That tells you about the type of customer who frequents the Lyons Corner House.'

'It happened so quickly! Annie was telling me about the menu they're choosing for the wedding breakfast when there was a dark flash in the corner of my eye. My handbag had been sitting on the chair next to me, you see. The next moment, a scruffy chap was running away with it in his hand! He was trying to get away as fast as he could, dodging between the tables. I really thought it was the last I'd see of my handbag. But can you believe it? A wonderful gentleman threw himself out of his seat and wrapped his arms around the man's legs! They both tumbled to the floor and some other customers helped restrain the man until the police got there. And I got my handbag back! I was extremely grateful because it had quite a bit of money in it. And I'm very fond of that bag. Do you recall you bought it for me when we were holidaying on the French Riviera? The one with the big gold clasp and the embossed flower design.'

'Oh, that one.' He didn't recall it.

'I was incredibly impressed by what the gentleman did. And even more so when I discovered he had a poorly leg. Apparently, he injured it during the war and has to walk with a stick these days.'

Anthony paused with his soup spoon halfway to his mouth. 'How old was he?'

'About forty.'

The description sounded remarkably like Fisher. What was the man doing drawing attention to himself like that?

'Did you speak to him?' he asked.

'Oh yes. I couldn't thank him enough. I offered him some money, but he wouldn't take it. We had quite a chat together afterwards.'

'Is that so? He sounds like a helpful gentleman indeed. Did you catch his name?'

'Albert Clark.'

At least the private detective had not been foolish enough to tell Charlotte his real name. But he was supposed to be secretly following her, not making himself obvious by coming to her aid in her hour of need. The saving grace was he had rescued Charlotte's precious handbag.

'I'm very pleased for you, my dear,' he said. 'It sounds like the fellow did an outstanding job.'

'I only wish he would have accepted a reward for it. But he was too gallant, I suppose. And quite handsome too.'

Anthony scraped his soup bowl noisily with his spoon. What was the use of employing a private detective to follow his wife about if she was going to be charmed by his looks and gallantry?

'I thought you'd be a little more pleased for me,' said Charlotte.

'I am pleased! And it's reassuring to know these handsome chaps are around to look after our wives when we're not there to do it ourselves.'

She laughed. 'If I didn't know you better, I'd say you were a little bit jealous, Anthony.'

'Jealous? Of a man with a walking stick sitting about in a Lyons Corner House? Don't be ridiculous, Charlotte.'

Chapter 33

'I'VE FOUND an address in the directory for a J Campbell in Wimbledon,' said Fred the next morning. 'It could be Jeffrey Campbell, the husband of Jemima Campbell, who worked with Miller and Gibson.'

'Thank you, Fred. It sounds like it could be them,' said Augusta. 'I'll pay Jemima Campbell a visit later today. Hopefully, she might tell me what happened between the two friends. I read a few more of John Gibson's letters last night, but he didn't mention Jemima in them.'

'Perhaps Miller believed what Gibson had told him about the boyfriend and that put an end to the conflict.'

'It's possible. Hopefully Jemima will tell me if they fell out with each other.'

A movement outside the window caught Augusta's eye. It was the same man who had peered in through the window a few days previously. He wore a flat cap, and a cigarette was stuck to his lip.

'Him again,' said Augusta.

'Who?' said Fred.

'I'm going to find out.'

As Augusta walked to the door, the man sauntered away. She left the shop and caught up with him outside in the street.

'Can I help you?' she said.

He wore a grubby shirt with no collar and his sleeves were rolled up, revealing muscular forearms.

'Maybe you can.' He pulled the cigarette from his lip and grinned, revealing a few remaining teeth. 'You paid a visit to my sister-in-law, Mary Connolly,' he said.

'Yes, I did.'

'My name's Tom Connolly. I'm Arthur's brother.'

Augusta realised this was the man who had paid Miller a visit. 'My condolences to you, Mr Connolly,' she said. 'I imagine your family has suffered enormously since the accident.'

'Yes, we have. And it didn't help that we didn't get any justice. But now I've learned Alexander Miller went missing. So maybe there was some justice in the end.' He raised a finger at her. 'But I don't see why you need to go bothering us about this. Miller needs to be forgotten about.'

'I can understand why you have strong feelings about Mr Miller.'

'Strong feelings? We hated the man. But don't start getting any ideas about that.'

'What do you mean?'

'We had nothing to do with him vanishing, if that's what you're thinking. I know we're easy people to point a finger at.'

'I'm not suggesting you had anything to do with it.'

'The police will think it. It doesn't take much for them to arrest us for something. It always happens to our family.'

'I'm not accusing your family of anything, Mr Connolly.'

'No? So why did you call on Mary? You asked her if any of us had seen Miller after the accident.'

'Because I heard from Miller's sister that you visited him.'

'From the way you were asking Mary questions, it sounds like you suspect I've done more than that.'

'No, I don't.'

'I don't believe you, Mrs Peel. All sorts of rumours are going to fly about now just because you've come asking questions about a man who's not been seen for ten years.'

'There's no need for any rumours to fly around, Mr Connolly. I was just interested to find out if anybody knew what had happened to Alexander Miller. I've spoken to lots of people, not just your sister-in-law.'

'Why are you bothering? He was a murderer.'

'I knew nothing about him when I first started investigating. And although I can understand why you call him a murderer, the coroner found it was an accident.'

'Forget what the coroner says, we all know it was murder. But most of all, we want to remember Arthur as he was. A brother and a husband. A father and a son. We don't need someone like you knocking on doors and bringing up things from the past. You've got no idea how hard it's been for Mary to get over this. All of this is none of your business. So keep your nose out of it.'

'I beg your pardon?' came Philip's voice from behind Augusta. She startled.

'Philip?' He joined her at her side.

'Did I hear you being rude to Mrs Peel just now?' he asked Mr Connolly.

'It's alright, Philip,' said Augusta. 'Tom Connolly was Arthur's brother. He's got every right to be upset about his death in the accident with Alexander Miller.'

'Yes, he has,' said Philip. 'But he doesn't have the right to be rude to a lady.'

'I wasn't being rude,' said Tom Connolly. 'I was giving her some advice.'

'And what advice is that?'

'To keep her nose out of our business.'

'Mrs Peel is a private investigator,' said Philip. 'She's conducting an investigation at the moment, and she needs to speak to a lot of people.'

'She upset my sister-in-law, Mary.'

'I apologise for doing that,' said Augusta. 'I didn't intend to upset your sister-in-law.'

'I don't think there's any need to apologise, Augusta,' said Philip. He addressed Mr Connolly. 'I know Mrs Peel well. She would have been perfectly polite and considerate about Mrs Connolly's feelings.'

Tom sneered. 'Are you a copper, by any chance?'

'Why do you ask that?'

'I can always tell a copper when I see one.'

'Which suggests to me you must have encountered quite a few in your time, Mr Connolly.'

'You are, aren't you? You're not denying it.'

'I'm a private detective, Mr Connolly. Until recently, I worked at Scotland Yard.'

'I knew it! You're both working for the police and you're going to blame my family for this. It always happens.'

'I don't think anybody suspected your family was behind it,' said Philip. 'Until now. I think you may be protesting a little too much, Mr Connolly. Perhaps that's because you know more than you're letting on?'

'I knew it!' Mr Connolly jabbed his finger at him. 'You're all the same. You've not heard the last of this.'

He turned and strolled away.

'I think he's been watching the shop for a while,' said Augusta. 'I saw him loitering outside the other day.'

'Where does he live?'

'Finchley.'

'Quite a distance to travel just to watch your shop, Augusta. I'll have a word with an inspector from S Division up there and see if someone will have a word with him. By the sound of it, they could already be familiar with the Connolly family.'

'Thank you for stepping in, Philip.'

'It seems you're being pestered by some odd characters, Augusta. First Robert Stanton, then Tom Connolly. And we can't forget Walter Ferguson, either. I'm going to visit the *London Weekly Chronicle* offices later and try again to have a word with the editor, Mr Baker.'

'Thank you, Philip. I suppose these people feel threatened. That's why they try to intimidate me.'

'And if they had nothing to hide, they wouldn't bother.'

They made their way back to Augusta's shop.

'I received a telephone call this morning from Mr Ramsden,' said Philip. 'His wife told him about the incident in Lyons Corner House.'

'I hope he was grateful to you. You apprehended a thief.'

'He thinks I was careless.'

'He wasn't grateful to you at all?'

'Only a little. He believes I seated myself too close to his wife and her friend. I told him I had a lot of experience in surveillance and that I hadn't seated myself too close at all. The thief just happened to run past my table. But Mr Ramsden is clearly the sort who thinks he knows best.'

'So he wants you to stop working for him?'

'No, he's given me one more chance.'

Augusta laughed. 'How generous of him.'

'And I agreed to it because the money is good. But if Charlotte Ramsden spots me again, then that will have to be the end of it.'

Chapter 34

AUGUSTA THOUGHT about Tom Connolly as she travelled by train from Waterloo station to the suburb of Wimbledon.

Could Tom Connolly have harmed Alexander Miller? He looked like the sort of man who would quickly turn to violence if he deemed it necessary. Even though he was in his sixties, his muscled arms hadn't escaped Augusta's notice. There was little doubt he would have been capable of harming someone ten years ago.

But Augusta had to remind herself she was in danger of passing judgement on him. His appearance and background made him an easy man to suspect. And he was clearly aware of it. He was a man with an air of criminality about him. But that didn't necessarily mean he was a murderer.

Jemima Campbell's home was a well-presented, semi-detached house a short walk from Wimbledon station. It was set back from the road with a well-tended front garden. Augusta guessed it had a sizeable garden at the rear too.

She took in a breath before approaching the house and enjoyed the clean summer air. London's suburbs lacked the excitement of the town, but Augusta could understand the appeal of living in places like this.

Jemima Campbell had dark, bobbed hair and dark eyes. She was beautiful, as Augusta had expected. But her eyes had a weariness about them, and she wore a drab apron over a plain day dress.

'Can I help you?'

'My name is Augusta Peel and I'm a private investigator. I'm investigating the disappearance of Alexander Miller.'

She blinked rapidly a few times. 'Alexander Miller?'

'Yes. Did you know him?'

A pause followed. As if Mrs Campbell was considering whether or not to admit to it.

'Yes, I did. I suppose you'd better come in.'

A short while later, Augusta sat with Mrs Campbell in a tidy, comfortable living room. Framed family photographs were arranged on top of an upright piano and a box of children's toys sat beneath the window. Mrs Campbell had made them both a cup of tea.

'It was many years ago,' she said. 'Ten years I suppose.'

'I've heard you worked with Alexander in the Great Western Railway accounts department.'

Mrs Campbell smiled. 'That's right. I did.'

'And his friend John Gibson.'

'And John, too. It was very sad… what happened to him.'

'Have you got any ideas on what could have happened to Alexander?'

'Alexander?' Her eyes widened. 'I heard he went away. His sister received a letter from him.'

'His sister believes the letter was forged.'

'Does she? I wouldn't know about that. I heard a letter had been received from him and so I assumed he'd moved away. It seemed a strange thing to do so suddenly and he didn't mention it to anyone. John was quite upset.'

'He tried to find Alexander, didn't he?'

'Yes. He did everything he could to find him. I don't think he believed the letter from him was real either.' She paused and took a sip of tea. 'I feel sad they're no longer around.'

'But Alexander could be somewhere, if you believe he wrote the letter to his sister.'

'Yes, I suppose he could be. But so much time has passed now. I feel sure I'll never see him again.'

'I read some letters which John wrote to his sister Louisa,' said Augusta. 'I really don't mean to make you feel uncomfortable when I say this Mrs Campbell. And I hope I'm not speaking out of turn. But it seems both Alexander and John had some affection for you.'

'Alexander did? I never knew about that.' Her face reddened and she bit her lip. 'As for John,' she continued, 'yes, I knew about that. We went out together a few times. It wasn't serious and nothing came of it. I actually met my husband Jeffrey a few months later. I was very sad when I heard about John's accident. Jeffrey helped me through that time.'

'I realise this isn't easy, Mrs Campbell, and I'm grateful you're happy to speak with me so frankly. Do you think there's any possibility John could have deliberately jumped in front of the train at Baker Street?'

'No.' She shook her head vehemently. 'None. John would never have done such a thing. It was an accident.'

'Or there's a possibility he was pushed?'

'No.' She shook her head again. 'He wasn't pushed.' Augusta wondered how she could be so sure.

'Did Alexander and John ever fall out with each other?'

'No. Sometimes there was rivalry between them, but it was friendly.'

'What sort of rivalry?'

'It was to do with cycling. Alexander could cycle faster than John and it annoyed John. It didn't help that Alexander liked to brag about it too. He took it quite seriously, and even took various tonics to help him.'

'Jackson's Blood Purifier?'

'That might have been one of them. I don't really recall.'

'It was mentioned in one of John's letters. From what I've read, he began taking it too, but it didn't improve his cycling.'

Jemima smiled. 'It was probably one of those nonsense remedies.'

'When was the last time you saw Alexander?'

'At work. I worked as a secretary for one of the directors in the accounts department. I would speak to John and Alexander quite regularly. I would help them when they were looking for certain files or if they needed an appointment to speak to the manager about something. It was just another ordinary day that day. We all left about five and I remember saying goodbye to Alexander and that was that. He seemed his normal self. Nothing was troubling him and he was in a good mood.'

'And you believe he moved away and the letter his sister received was from him.'

'Only because I don't like the thought of something horrible having happened to him. I want to believe he moved away. Even though it seems unlikely... it's been what I've wanted to think for all these years.'

Chapter 35

JEMIMA'S HANDS trembled as she untied her apron and readied herself to collect her children from school.

Mrs Peel's visit hadn't been a surprise. When she had read the newspaper report about the letter being found, her stomach had turned. She had told her husband that she felt unwell and gone to bed for most of the day.

Since then, unpleasant memories had returned. Thoughts she couldn't control. Her husband had noticed something was wrong and she had tried to reassure him she was alright.

He had no idea what had happened with Alexander. She hadn't told anyone. Nor was she going to. Some secrets had to remain buried forever.

Jemima checked her appearance in the hallway mirror, then left the house.

Chapter 36

WHEN AUGUSTA RETURNED to her flat that evening with Sparky, she found the door unlocked.

'That's funny,' she said to the canary. 'I could have sworn I locked the door this morning.'

She paused and thought about it some more. She couldn't specifically remember locking the door when she had left that morning, but it was something she automatically did. Deciding she was being forgetful, she opened the door and stepped into the flat.

Everything was in disarray. The sofa cushions had been thrown onto the floor. Cupboards and drawers hung open.

There was little of much value in the flat apart from a few pieces of moderately-priced jewellery. Augusta turned to make her way to the bedroom when a dark figure leapt out from behind the armchair and dashed out of the door.

'Wait!' she called out. But she knew he had no intention of doing so. She placed Sparky's cage on the dining table and ran after the man. At the top of the stairs, she could hear his footsteps thundering down the flight beneath her. She took off after him, taking two or three steps at a time and taking care not to fall.

Outside on Marchmont Street, she saw him running north in the direction of Euston Road. She followed as fast as she could, dodging people as she went.

Who was he? And what had he taken?

At the top of Marchmont Street, he turned right into Compton Street, and Augusta tried to keep him in her sight. At the corner by the hospital, he turned left up Judd Street. Augusta was breathing quickly now and her legs were tiring. She knew she had little chance of catching up with the man, but she wanted to see where he went.

Up ahead, at the end of the street, rose the tall edifice of the Grand Midland Hotel. Its red-brick spires speared the sky like the roof of a cathedral.

There were three railway stations close by: Euston, St Pancras, and King's Cross. Was the man planning a getaway on a train? At the top of Judd Street, he turned right. She willed her legs to move faster as she ran up to Euston Road. Her throat was dry, and she felt a burning sensation in her legs and chest. She knew Euston Road would be busy. It would be easy to lose sight of him there.

At Euston Road, Augusta slowed and caught sight of the man dashing across the road towards King's Cross station. With a fresh burst of exertion, she followed as fast as she could. She crossed Euston Road, dodging the vehicles and ignoring the beep of a horn.

The man headed for the entrance to the underground. It was a flight of steps leading down from the street, marked with a wrought-iron overhead sign. A moment later, the man had vanished down the steps.

Augusta reached the underground entrance, gasping for breath. Her head spun as she negotiated the steep, tiled steps to the ticket hall.

She felt light-headed from the exertion as she paused in the ticket hall. It was busy and the ticket office had a long queue.

There was no sign of the man. She approached the ticket inspector.

'Did you see a man in a dark suit run through here just now?'

'I might have done. Lots of folk are in a hurry.'

'He took something from me. Did he have something in his hand?'

'Not that I noticed.' A man pushed past her, holding out his ticket for inspection. Augusta moved out of the way as the ticket inspector busied himself with the passengers passing through.

Augusta recovered her breath and reluctantly realised she had lost the man who had been in her flat.

All she could do now was return home and call the police.

Chapter 37

AUGUSTA TELEPHONED PHILIP FIRST. Fortunately, he was still in his office and hadn't left for home yet. Then she let Sparky out of his cage and telephoned the local police station.

Tears pricked her eyes as she waited for Philip to arrive. Her flat was in a mess. How could someone show so little regard for someone else's home? It was only a small flat and the intruder probably wouldn't have been there for long. There were just a few rooms: the living area, the little kitchen, her bedroom, and the bathroom. The chest of drawers in her bedroom had been emptied, and the clothes pulled out of her wardrobe. In the living area, paper, pens, and books were scattered all over the floor. If the intruder had been looking for valuable items, then he would have been disappointed. But as she began to tidy up, Augusta realised what he had taken.

The bundle of John Gibson's letters was missing. She had kept it in a drawer in her writing desk in the living area. The drawer now lay empty on the floor, her belongings scattered around it.

Philip arrived at her flat a short while later.

'What's been taken?' he asked as he surveyed the mess.

'John Gibson's letters. Nothing else seems to be missing. Someone knew the letters were here, Philip!'

'Who knew you had them?'

'Louisa Bradshaw because she lent them to me. I mentioned them to Jane Stanton, but I didn't admit I had them. You knew they were here. And Fred. And that's all.'

'I think we can rule me and Fred out,' said Philip as he looked around. 'How did the intruder get in?'

'He must have picked the lock. The door was unlocked when I got here.' Philip stepped over to the door. 'An easy lock to pick, we should change this for a better one.'

Augusta continued to tidy up as Philip looked around. 'We could check everywhere for fingerprints,' he said. 'But if the intruder planned this carefully, then he would have been wearing gloves. Did you see if he was wearing gloves, Augusta?'

'No, I didn't.' She knelt by the coffee table and picked up pens and pencils from the floor.

'What did he look like?'

'I never got close enough to see. He wore a dark suit. And he had dark hair.'

'Age?'

'I don't know. He could have been anything between twenty-five and forty-five.'

'Height?'

'I really couldn't say. Not tall, not short. Average.'

'Build?'

'Average.'

Philip sighed. 'That doesn't exactly narrow things down.'

Augusta felt a snap of irritation. 'Well, I'm sorry if I can't give you a better answer than that!'

'I wasn't suggesting... oh, I'm sorry, Augusta. It's just a habit of mine to ask questions like that. Come on.' He stepped over to her. 'Why don't you get up from the floor and sit in a chair. I'll get you a drink.'

'I need to tidy up.'

'Not immediately, you don't. Just take a few moments to recover. And besides, the police need to see what the intruder did to your flat.'

'I don't know why I bothered calling them. I can't give them a decent description of him. They've got no chance of finding him. Especially as he got away on the tube. He could be anywhere now.'

Philip held out a hand to help Augusta to her feet.

'Thank you, Philip.'

He said nothing, but held her gaze.

For a moment, she wondered if he was about to embrace her. But then he hurriedly glanced away.

'Anyway, why don't you sit yourself down, Augusta?'

'Yes. Good idea.' She felt a flush of warmth in her face from the moment which had just passed between them.

'I'll pour us some brandy,' he said.

'That would be perfect.'

A constable arrived while Philip was making the drinks. He was a pale-faced young man with flaxen hair.

'The intruder stole some letters,' Augusta explained to him.

'What sort of letters?'

'Someone lent them to me. I'm working on an investigation into the disappearance of someone ten years ago. I was given a bundle of letters which had useful information in them. But someone has broken in and taken them.'

'You're a private detective, Mrs Peel?'

'Yes. And I also run a bookshop.'

The constable pulled a puzzled expression as he made

some notes in his notebook. 'So the intruder stole the letters which discussed the disappearance of a man ten years ago?' he said.

'Yes. It must have been someone who knows I'm investigating the case. They clearly don't want me to find out the truth. And I think that proves Alexander Miller came to harm.'

'Who's Alexander Miller?'

'He's the chap who disappeared ten years ago,' said Philip. 'No one knows what happened to him but, as Mrs Peel has just pointed out, someone clearly knows she's investigating his disappearance, and they must be worried Mrs Peel is going to discover something. That's why they've taken the letters.'

Augusta had a sudden thought. 'Perhaps it was Walter Ferguson!'

'Did the intruder look like Ferguson?' asked Philip.

'No. But he could have sent someone else here to take the letters.'

'Who's Walter Ferguson?' asked the constable.

'A reporter for the *London Weekly Chronicle*,' said Augusta. 'He's waging a vendetta against me. It wouldn't surprise me if he asked someone to break into my flat. I don't think he could have had anything to do with Mr Miller's disappearance. But I'm suspicious of him all the same.'

Philip turned to the constable. 'I think it would be a good idea to have a word with him.'

'Of course.' The constable made a note. 'Anyone else we should consider?'

'There's Mr and Mrs Stanton,' said Augusta.

'And who are they?'

'Jane Stanton is Alexander Miller's sister. One of the letters revealed she owed her brother money. She told me she wanted the letters destroyed, but she didn't know I had them.'

'Perhaps she asked Mrs Bradshaw about them, and Mrs Bradshaw told her she'd lent them to you, Augusta,' said Philip.

'That's a good suggestion, Philip. It could have happened.' She turned to the constable. 'Mr and Mrs Stanton live at number 15 Baker Street.'

'Perhaps the intruder was Mr Stanton?' said Philip.

'No. I don't think Mr Stanton could run that fast.'

'You chased after the man, Mrs Peel?' asked the constable.

'Yes. I lost him in the ticket hall of King's Cross underground station.'

The constable made more notes.

'All of this is connected,' said Augusta.

'What do you mean?'

'This is all to do with Alexander Miller's disappearance. Someone was behind it, that's why they forged a letter from him to his sister. Constable Simpson at Crawford Place police station has the letter. Whoever was behind that letter knows I'm investigating Miller's disappearance now. They knew I had the letters. But who is it? It's reached the stage where Scotland Yard needs to get involved.'

'The Yard?' said the constable. 'Let me make some more enquiries of my own first, Mrs Peel.'

Augusta turned to Philip. 'Can't you speak to someone there?'

'I can try.'

The constable frowned. 'I would like to make some more enquiries first.'

'Mrs Peel is asking me because I used to be a detective inspector at the Yard.'

'Oh. I didn't realise, sir. My apologies.'

'For what? You've done a good job so far this evening. Continue with your enquiries and let me know how you get on.' Philip pulled his card out of his jacket pocket and handed it to the constable.

'I will do, sir.'

After the constable had left, Philip helped Augusta tidy the rest of the flat.

'Who's this chap?' he asked as he picked up some photographs of a young man from the floor.

Augusta felt her heart skip. 'Just someone I knew before the war.' She held out her hand for the photographs, not wishing to be asked any more questions.

'Oh.' He handed them to her. 'How about I make us some cocoa?' he said. 'And then you need to lie down and get some rest.'

'Sparky needs something to eat.'

'I can help with that, too. And by the way, I managed to speak to Mr Baker, the editor at the *London Weekly Chronicle*.'

'What did he say about the article?'

'He says he's going to discuss it with Ferguson.'

'So it might still be published?'

'Possibly.'

Augusta sighed.

'I warned him he would find himself in trouble if he printed an article with confidential information in it,' said Philip. 'And I told him he needs to ensure his reporters are working within the law.'

'And what did he say?'

'Not a lot. He seems half-asleep most of the time. He's an infuriating man. But although it's not the news we were hoping for, I'm hoping my word with him today will have delayed the publication a little.' Philip glanced around the living room. 'How comfortable is your sofa, Augusta?'

The question puzzled her. 'Comfortable. You've sat on it several times.'

'I mean for sleeping.'

'Sleeping on the sofa?'

'Yes. That's what I plan to do tonight if it's alright with you, Augusta. I don't want to leave you here on your own. And tomorrow, I'll help you get a better lock fitted on your door.'

Chapter 38

'WHEN DID you last see Mr Alexander Miller?' asked Sergeant Ridley.

Tom Connolly gave a groan and slumped back in his chair in the interview room of Finchley police station. The spartan room was familiar to him. 'Everyone knows when I last saw him.'

'Everyone?'

'I've gone over this before, Sergeant.' He pulled the cigarette stub from his lip and pressed it into the ashtray in front of him. 'I know it wasn't right what I did, but I'm a man who admits what he's done. You know that about me, don't you?'

'I know you quite well, Mr Connolly.'

'So I went to see Miller after they said my brother's death was an accident. It wasn't an accident, he should have stood trial for what happened.' He felt the anger stir in his chest again.

'What did you say to Mr Miller?'

'I had a few words with him.'

'What sort of words?'

'What sort of words do you think? I can't remember exactly what I said because it was years ago. But I was angry he wasn't charged for murdering my brother. So that gives you an idea of what I said.'

He lit a thin cigarette which he had rolled earlier that morning.

'The coroner ruled your brother's death was an accident, so no one could be charged for his murder.'

'That's what he said. But my family thinks different.'

'So you told Mr Miller how you felt about the coroner's verdict.'

'That's right. I wanted justice to be done.'

'What do you mean by that comment?'

'Exactly what I said.'

'So, did you make sure justice was done?'

'I spoke to him.'

'Anything else?'

'No, that was all. I just had a word and left it at that. But I wanted him to be looking over his shoulder.'

'You threatened him?'

'Like I said, I wanted him looking over his shoulder. I didn't want him getting on with the rest of his life without a care in the world. I wanted him to suffer. Just like my family suffered.'

Sergeant Ridley frowned.

'I know what it looks like, Sergeant. I'm being honest with you. If I sat here and told you I liked the man, you would know I was lying, wouldn't you? I'm telling you the truth. You like to hear the truth from me, don't you?'

'I do. Mr Miller disappeared a year after the accident in which your brother died. Did you have anything to do with that?'

'No. I never knew Miller disappeared until the other day. How could I have had anything to do with it?'

'You wanted him to face justice.'

Tom sighed. 'This is exactly what I knew would happen. You're going to blame me for him going missing. Maybe he just went off somewhere? I had nothing to do with it. But I'll be honest with you again, Sergeant. I hope someone harmed him.'

'Can you recall what you were doing on Friday the 1st and Saturday 2nd July 1911?'

Tom laughed out a cloud of tobacco smoke. 'No, couldn't tell you at all.'

'If you kept any sort of diary—'

'Do I look like the sort of man who keeps a diary, Sergeant?'

'Can you remember who you were associating with back then? They could provide you with an alibi.'

'I don't need an alibi because I did nothing wrong on those dates. You know who my associates are, they've not changed in ten years. You could ask them yourself.'

Tom knew it was highly unlikely any of his friends could remember what they had been doing then.

Sergeant Ridley looked down at his notes and frowned some more. 'This is an odd question to ask you, Mr Connolly,' he said. 'But I've been told to ask it. Do you own a typewriter?'

'What do you think, Sergeant?'

'Did you know anyone with a typewriter ten years ago?'

'Who told you to ask me this?'

'Can you answer my question?'

'No, I never had a use for a typewriter in all my sixty-seven years.'

Sergeant Ridley made some lengthy notes.

Tom broke the silence. 'So what does all this mean, Sergeant? What happens now?'

'I'll discuss it with my inspector.'

'But you can see I'm innocent?'

'Innocent isn't a word I associate with you, Mr Connolly.'

'But I did nothing to him!'

Chapter 39

Augusta told Fred about the intruder in her flat.

'How frightening!' he said. 'You must have found it difficult to sleep last night.'

'It wasn't easy. But it helped that Philip was there.' As Fred's jaw dropped, Augusta realised she had to clarify this. 'He slept on the sofa.'

'Oh, I see.'

'There's no scandal to report, Fred!' She felt heat in her face.

'I believe you.' He smiled. 'And Sparky was your chaperone, wasn't he?'

'Absolutely.' She laughed.

'I hope the police catch the intruder,' said Fred. 'I wonder who he was?'

'He didn't look familiar. I think someone sent him. Perhaps it was the Stantons. Maybe it was the Connollys. Walter Ferguson even.' She shuddered. 'I don't like dwelling on it too much.'

The ring of the telephone interrupted them.

Augusta answered.

'I can't speak long,' said the voice on the other end. 'It's Louisa Bradshaw.'

'Mrs Bradshaw! Are you alright?'

'Yes. I'm sorry I didn't agree to see you the other day.'

'That's fine. As long as you're alright, it doesn't matter.'

'I'm sort of alright. The trouble is… I've been threatened.'

Augusta felt a chill run through her. 'What happened?'

'I received an anonymous letter warning me not to speak to anyone about my brother.'

'But that's dreadful! Have you told the police?'

'No. The letter told me not to.'

'But you can do so if you're careful about it—'

'I'd rather not. I have a family. I'm worried about their safety. I'm sure you understand.'

'Of course.'

'I think you need to be careful too, Mrs Peel. This letter… it was horrible.'

'You still have it?'

'Yes. But I can't bring myself to look at it again.'

'I'm sorry that I caused this.'

'It's not your fault, Mrs Peel.'

'If you hadn't spoken to me about your brother, then you'd have been left alone.'

'I don't know about that. I think I probably brought it upon myself when I decided it would make an interesting news story. The person behind this probably read about it in the newspaper.'

'Of course. And they found out your name from the article and knew where to find you.'

'I would never have done it if I'd known it was dangerous!'

'The sooner they catch this person, the better. I'm afraid I have some more bad news for you, Mrs Bradshaw. Your brother's letters were stolen from my flat last night.'

'Oh no! Are you alright?'

'I'm fine. But obviously I don't know if we'll see those letters again and I realise they're valuable to you.'

'I don't know about that. My brother's letters seem to be causing nothing but trouble. Please don't worry about their loss, Mrs Peel. I need to go. I'm worried that telephoning you might be dangerous, too.'

'Just a quick question, if I may. Have Mr or Mrs Stanton visited you?'

'Yes. Jane Stanton called on me yesterday. My housekeeper spoke to her, and she requested to see the letters. My housekeeper... oh, I've just realised what's happened. My housekeeper told her I'd lent them to you. I'm sorry, Mrs Peel.'

'Don't be. We'll find out who's behind this. I promise. And hopefully it won't be long before you're no longer in danger.'

'Please be careful, Mrs Peel.'

Chapter 40

'I'll speak to someone at the Yard,' said Philip once Augusta had told him about Louisa Bradshaw's telephone call. 'This needs a properly coordinated investigation now.'

'But no one can contact Louisa Bradshaw directly,' said Augusta. 'She's worried about her family.'

'Fair enough,' said Philip. 'At least we're aware of the threat now. I only wish she'd told you sooner. Then you could have kept those letters somewhere safer. This person has clearly done a very good job of intimidating Mrs Bradshaw. Perhaps they have no intention of actually harming her, but it's enough to silence her. And all she has done is speak to you and lend you her brother's letters, Augusta.'

'The person behind this has to be the person responsible for Alexander Miller's disappearance. And they could have pushed John Gibson beneath a train at Baker Street. Who is it?'

Philip got up from his desk. 'I think the blackboard could come in useful now.' He walked over to it and picked up a piece of chalk. 'So who have we got? Let's start with

Jane and Robert Stanton.' He wrote their names on the board.

'Both benefitted from Alexander Miller's disappearance,' said Augusta. 'They inherited his estate and live in his spacious Baker Street flat. A much nicer flat than the house they were in before in Camden Town.'

'So they could have murdered him for his estate,' said Philip.

'And Jane owed her brother money at the time of his death. We don't know how much, but it was enough for him to complain to his friend, John Gibson, that she hadn't repaid him. Perhaps they murdered him so they didn't have to repay the debt.'

'Callous but possible,' said Philip. 'The pair of them are materially better off now Alexander is no longer around.'

'And the intruder stole the letters from my flat after Louisa Bradshaw's housekeeper told Jane Stanton that I had them. Mrs Stanton was quite clear about wanting to get her hands on those letters.'

'She's a strong suspect then. Who else have we got?'

'John Gibson could have harmed Miller.'

Philip wrote his name on the board. 'The motive being he was a love rival?'

'Yes. Although I can't find any evidence the friends fell out over it. The letters could have told me more but I didn't get the chance to finish reading them.'

'And we would struggle to prove Gibson was the murderer because he died later the same year,' said Philip. 'It's a possibility though. Who's next? The Connolly family.' He made another note on the blackboard.

'They could have murdered Miller in revenge for the accident in which Arthur Connolly was killed.'

'I wouldn't put it past them.'

'They're almost too obvious though, aren't they?'

'We know the family has been involved in criminality. Sergeant Ridley in Finchley told me all about the chat he had with Tom Connolly.'

'How did he get on?'

'Tom Connolly denies it all of course, but Sergeant Ridley agrees he could be a suspect. He's been in trouble for violence in the past. He and his family may be obvious suspects but often the simplest explanation is the correct one. Who else?'

'This is an odd one and I feel reluctant suggesting this person. But there was something not quite right about her.'

'Who?'

'Jemima Campbell.'

'The love triangle lady?'

'She was very nice and seemingly helpful. But there was something which didn't seem right. As if she wasn't being completely truthful. And she told me she'd always assumed Miller had left to start a new life. It's odd she thought that, because no one else did.'

Philip wrote her name on the board. 'And what could her motive have been?'

'I don't know. She had a brief relationship with Gibson after Miller went missing, but I can't work out a motive from that. It's something I'll have to think about some more.'

'Interesting. So what next, Augusta?'

'The Stantons bother me the most. Perhaps they sent that threat to Louisa Bradshaw. And sent a man to my flat to get the letters.'

'It's possible. Do you think they're both in on it?'

'Jane Stanton is a definite suspect in my mind. I'm less sure about Robert Stanton, but I dislike the man.'

'I could ask someone to search their home for the letters.'

'I don't think they'll be there. Jane Stanton only wanted to get her hands on those letters so she could destroy them.' Augusta checked her watch. 'I need to get home for the locksmith.'

'Yes, of course. Tell him you need two locks. Actually, three. And then I'm sure you'll sleep a little better tonight, Augusta.'

'Thank you Philip. I hope so.'

Chapter 41

Mary Connolly put her mending away and got up from her chair. It was time to get ready for bed.

The kitchen door swung open and her brother-in-law lurched in.

'Tom! You half-scared me to death!'

He sank into the chair she had just been sitting in. His eyes were rimmed with red and he smelt of beer. She was struck for a moment by how much he resembled his brother. This was how Arthur had come home every evening. It was unlike Tom to drink much though.

'What's happened?' she asked.

'The police are onto me again, Mary.'

'Oh no! What have they said?'

'They think I had something to do with Miller going missing. It doesn't matter what I tell them, they never believe me. Mrs Peel put them onto me.'

'How do you know that?'

'Because I happened to speak to her in the street. And the next thing I knew, Sergeant Ridley took me down to the station.'

'Not again. Where did you see her in the street?'

'I was watching her shop.'

Mary sighed. 'That's asking for trouble, Tom. Why'd you do it?'

'I wanted to find out more about her. It turns out she has an ex-copper for a friend. If she comes round here again, you don't speak to her. Do you understand me, Mary?'

'Fine. I won't.' Mary had liked Mrs Peel. But having now learned of her connections to the police, Mary knew she had to be careful.

'If she wants to talk about Miller, you send her to me. Is that clear?'

'It's clear, Tom. But you'll only get yourself in trouble with her again if I do that.'

'Better that I'm in trouble, than you, Mary. I can handle it.'

'Alright then. Why don't you get yourself home now, Tom? You need some rest.'

He swayed as he got to his feet. She didn't often see him like this. Something was clearly bothering him.

'I'll show them, Mary,' he said.

'Show who? What?'

'You'll see.'

Chapter 42

'HAVE you seen the newspapers this morning, Augusta?' said Fred when she arrived at her shop the following day.

She froze. 'Walter Ferguson's published his article?'

'No. A lady had a fatal fall from her flat in Baker Street last night.'

Augusta placed Sparky's cage on the counter and peered over Fred's shoulder at the newspaper report. 'It's not...'

'It is,' said Fred. 'Jane Stanton.'

Augusta leant on the counter for support. A wave of nausea washed over her. 'Jane Stanton?'

'I suppose there could be more than one Jane Stanton living on Baker Street. This Jane lived at number fifteen.'

'It's her.'

'Are you alright, Augusta?' asked Fred.

'It's just a shock. I'll be alright in a moment.'

'Can I get you some sugary tea?'

'Thank you, that will help a lot. But tell me what happened first.'

'It doesn't say much more. It only happened last night, so I suppose there wasn't a lot of information when this edition went to print. It says that Jane Stanton, aged forty, was found on the pavement on Baker Street shortly after half-past eight yesterday evening. It's believed she fell from her third-floor flat.'

'How?' Augusta tried to comprehend this. 'Did she do it on purpose? Was it an accident? How could it even be an accident? Do people accidentally fall out of windows?'

'Sometimes they do. But only if they're putting themselves in danger by leaning out precariously.'

Augusta shuddered. 'Perhaps she was pushed?'

Philip told Augusta more later that morning. 'I telephoned your friend, Inspector Whitman, at Crawford Place police station,' he said. 'They're examining the flat and speaking with Mr Stanton to find out exactly what happened.'

'Was Mr Stanton in the flat at the time?'

'No, apparently he was elsewhere.'

'Do you think someone could have pushed her?'

'It's too early to say, Augusta. D Division are trying to find witnesses at the moment.'

'But it can't have been an accident, can it?'

'Who knows? Perhaps Mrs Stanton leaned out of the window for some reason and lost her balance. Or maybe she jumped deliberately.'

Augusta shuddered. 'I hope this has nothing to do with our investigation,' she said. 'I already feel guilty about Louisa Bradshaw being threatened. And now this!'

'It may have nothing to do with it, Augusta. I'll keep in touch with Whitman and make sure we can get updates on what's happened. We need to wait and see how he gets on. He's asked Scotland Yard for help.'

'So where was Robert Stanton at the time?'

'I don't know. Presumably he has an alibi, but I feel confident he'll be properly questioned all the same.'

Chapter 43

ROBERT STANTON GLARED at the two men opposite him. Inspector Whitman was a lean-faced man with a thick grey moustache. Next to him sat a boy-faced detective from Scotland Yard. His name was Detective Sergeant Joyce, and he had fair hair and a sparse moustache.

'I don't know why you've got me here,' said Robert. 'It's quite obvious I had nothing to do with this.'

'We need your help,' said Inspector Whitman.

'Then why am I in the police station being treated like a suspect?'

'Because it's the easiest way to speak to you.'

'My wife has just died!'

'We'll make this as quick as possible. Do you believe your wife could have deliberately harmed herself?'

He couldn't bear the suggestion Jane would have jumped deliberately. 'No, that's impossible!'

'And why do you say that?'

'Because she was my wife! Isn't it obvious? I knew her better than anyone. She would never have done such a thing!'

The Scotland Yard detective raised his palms, as if trying to calm the situation. 'We're just trying to establish what happened, Mr Stanton. We apologise if it's upsetting for you. What do you think caused your wife's fall?'

'She leaned out too far. That can be the only explanation.'

'Was she in the habit of leaning out of the window?'

'I wouldn't call it a habit, but she liked to look out sometimes. She liked the view over the street. I've always found it rather noisy, and the air is dirty. But it was a good vantage point to see what was going on.'

'So your wife would regularly look out at the street from the window?'

'Yes.'

'And lean out of the window?'

'A little. But not so much that there was a chance of falling.'

Detective Sergeant Joyce made some notes, then cleared his throat. 'Was your marriage happy, Mr Stanton?'

'Yes! And I find that question rather personal.'

'I realise that. It's not a polite question to ask, and under normal circumstances, I wouldn't be asking it. But you must understand why I need to. I need to establish all was well between the pair of you.'

'And if I suggested it wasn't, you would assume I pushed her out of the window. Am I right?'

'Not necessarily, Mr Stanton. We just need to understand everything we possibly can. And it's important you're honest with us.'

'Why wouldn't I be?'

'When did you last see your wife?'

'When I left home yesterday evening. We dined together. We had a piece of cold beef brisket with some vegetables. And then I went to meet a friend at the West-moreland Arms. I've already told Inspector Whitman this, and he has the name of my friend.'

'What time did you meet your friend?'

'I got to the pub for eight o'clock.'

'Did you notice anyone suspicious loitering in or near your home when you left?'

'No. If I had, then I would have reported it by now.'

'I realise that, Mr Stanton. But I urge you to have another think about it. Sometimes when we cast our minds back, we might remember a detail that we'd forgotten. It's possible the assailant blended into his surroundings and you didn't give him a second glance.'

'I would know if I saw someone suspicious. I don't think anyone attacked Jane. I think this was an accident.'

'How easy is it for a visitor to gain access to the building you live in?'

'Very easy. They just walk in through the door.'

'Then climb three flights of stairs to your flat.'

'Yes. But what does this have to do with anything? Jane fell by accident!'

'Do you know of anyone who could have wished to harm your wife?'

Robert couldn't help but laugh at the ridiculous nature of the question. 'No one! Jane had no enemies at all. She led a quiet existence. She had some good friends at church. And she enjoyed reading, cooking, and needlework. She was a good wife, and I was lucky to have her. I have never known her to have a cross word with anyone.'

'Including yourself?' asked Inspector Whitman. Robert didn't like the way he folded his arms.

'Our marriage was happy, but it was also ordinary.' He knew he would look suspicious if he tried to pretend everything had been perfect. 'And in an ordinary marriage, sometimes a husband and a wife exchange a few words that aren't entirely complimentary. Are you a married man, Inspector?'

'I am.'

'Then you know exactly what I mean.'

'So you're telling us, Mr Stanton, that you and your wife exchanged cross words occasionally, but your marriage was happy,' said the young detective.

'That's exactly what I'm telling you. Nothing out of the ordinary ever happened to us.'

'Apart from the mysterious disappearance of your brother-in-law.'

'But that was some time ago. And has nothing to do with what's happened to Jane.'

'Can you be sure about that, Mr Stanton?'

'Completely sure! Alexander vanished ten years ago.'

'Do you think someone harmed Alexander Miller?'

'They must have done. It explains why my wife received a strange letter from someone claiming to be him.'

'Perhaps the same person also harmed your wife.'

'Impossible! The events are ten years apart. This has nothing to do with what happened to Alexander.'

'What makes you so sure?'

'Because no one harmed Jane. She fell in an accident.'

'You seem rather sure about that, Mr Stanton.'

'Because she was my wife. I knew her! And no one would have harmed her.'

'Even though someone harmed her brother?'

'There is no connection whatsoever. How many times must I repeat myself?'

'How much money did your wife owe her brother at the time of his disappearance?' asked Detective Sergeant Joyce.

Robert gave a laugh and wiped his brow. 'Not this again. Why is this relevant to Jane's accident?'

'It will help your cause if you answer our questions, Mr Stanton.'

'Fine. I understand Alexander lent Jane some money. But I couldn't tell you how much. It was a private arrangement between them.'

'Surely you earn a good salary in your job at the bank, Mr Stanton?'

'Yes, I do.'

'And so you were more than able to provide for your wife.'

'Yes, I was perfectly able to provide for the both of us. So now you're going to ask me why she borrowed money from her brother, aren't you? The answer to that is I really don't know. Like I said, it was between Jane and Alexander. It was nothing to do with me. I don't know what she needed the money for.'

'Do you think it's odd your wife borrowed money from her brother when your salary was adequate for the pair of you?'

'Possibly. But it was ten years ago. I really can't see how it can be explained now.'

'Can you guess why your wife would have needed that money?'

'I'm totally unable to, I'm afraid. I really don't know.' He wasn't going to admit his gambling and investment losses to the police. It would give them yet another reason to poke around in his business. 'Perhaps my wife was helping a friend in need,' he said. 'A friend in an embarrassing situation perhaps, and she didn't want to tell me about it.' He threw up his hands in exasperation. 'I don't have any answers to this. It's no use you asking me the same question over and over. I don't know why Jane borrowed the money and I don't know how much it was.'

'Alexander Miller's death meant the debt no longer needed to be repaid, did it?'

'That's right. He died with the debt left unsettled.'

'And while your wife Jane was no doubt very upset about his disappearance, it was also convenient for her.'

'That's a strange way of describing the situation, Detective. I know for a fact that her debt to her brother never entered her mind after he disappeared. She was merely worried about his safety and nothing else. She never once rejoiced in the fact she didn't have to repay him the money. It was a very difficult time for the pair of us. We moved into Alexander's flat a couple of months after his disappearance because it needed looking after. But Jane had to wait seven years before she could apply to a court to receive the probate from his will.'

'She gained materially from his death.'

'Because she was the next of kin. Now if you're suggesting Jane had anything to do with her brother's disappearance, then I find your suggestion offensive, Detective. I will not entertain the idea that my wife could have harmed her brother just because she owed him some money. That's quite ridiculous.'

'Or perhaps it was you who harmed Alexander Miller on your wife's behalf?' said Detective Sergeant Joyce. 'Perhaps he was pestering her for the money to be repaid? It clearly bothered him because he mentioned it to his friend. Perhaps the pair of you came up with a solution to silence him?'

'No!' Robert slammed his palm down on the table. 'That is nonsense, Detective. Pure nonsense!'

Chapter 44

AUGUSTA RUBBED at the sticky marks on the cover of *The Phoenix and the Carpet* by E. Nesbit. Fortunately, a little soap was enough to remove them so she didn't have to resort to anything stronger. The book cover had an attractive embossed design of blue, red, and gold and she felt hopeful she could restore it to its former glory.

Some pages in the book were torn, but they were all present. It would take a while to patch up the pages, but Augusta felt it was a worthwhile task. And it was a welcome distraction from the shocking news of Jane Stanton's death.

Please be careful, Mrs Peel. Louisa Bradshaw's warning echoed in Augusta's ears. A cold fear niggled her, and she did her best to ignore it. She didn't want to admit to herself that she felt frightened.

But a man had broken into her flat. Mrs Bradshaw had been threatened. And now Mrs Stanton had been murdered. Who was behind this? And what could they be planning next?

Augusta had assumed Mrs Stanton had ordered

someone to steal the letters from her flat. But that seemed impossible now. What about Robert Stanton? Had he ordered the burglary? Had he murdered his wife?

The more Augusta considered the case, the more confused she felt. Could Tom Connolly be the mastermind behind it all? Having met him, she doubted it. But she had been proven wrong in the past.

Philip called on her late that afternoon. His expression was despondent as he perched himself on a stool by her workbench.

'I'm going to inform Mr Ramsden that I can no longer work for him. His wife spotted me again today.'

'Oh no. How?'

'In a department store on Oxford Street. I don't think I've ever spent so much time loitering about in shops on Oxford Street. Charlotte Ramsden was speaking to a sales assistant about dining sets. I was hiding as best I could and pretended to be examining some tea towels. When the conversation between Mrs Ramsden and the sales assistant ended, she unfortunately headed straight for the tea towels. I couldn't get away quickly enough, so there she found me.'

'Looking at tea towels?'

'Yes. They're not things I've paid much attention to in the past. But since my wife left, I've had to acquaint myself with them and many other household items. Anyway, she was surprised to see me there and thought it amusing that I was looking at tea towels. I told her I was trying to buy a present for my wife. And she told me there are better presents to buy a wife than tea towels. Now she probably thinks I'm a dull husband who buys his wife tea towels as a gift. Anyway, she chatted away to me and I had to oblige.'

'Do you think she was suspicious about seeing you again?'

'No, I don't think so. But this can't happen again. If

she sees me a third time, then she will realise something is up. Mr Ramsden gave me one more chance and I've blown it. So this is it. I have to stop doing the job. I can't say I'm too sorry about it because it's been incredibly boring. And I can assure Mr Ramsden that I've found no evidence of his wife having an affair.' He sighed. 'I feel like I've failed, Augusta. I managed to spend a couple of years working undercover in Belgium, speaking different languages, and working in extremely dangerous conditions. And yet I haven't managed to follow a lady around London for a couple of weeks without breaking my cover. Perhaps I've lost my touch.'

'No, you haven't. It's only because you intervened when the thief tried to take her bag. People remember that sort of thing. And she clearly has a good memory for faces. I'm sure another case is going to come along which will be far more interesting.'

'Yes, I hope so. Is that my telephone ringing upstairs?'

'I'll answer it for you,' said Augusta. She could get up the stairs much faster than Philip.

'Thank you, Augusta. I'll follow hot on your heels.'

She dashed off and was relieved to get to the telephone before the caller gave up.

'This is Detective Sergeant Joyce,' he said. 'May I speak with Mr Fisher?'

'Certainly. He's just on his way.'

Philip arrived in his office, having made his way up the stairs with his walking stick. He took the telephone receiver from Augusta, and she sat in one of the easy chairs as he spoke to the Scotland Yard detective.

'That was Joyce,' he said as he put the receiver down.

'I know. I answered it.' She smiled.

'Oh yes, of course. He's interviewed Robert Stanton

today and he's unsure what to make of him. Stanton is adamant his wife's death was an accident.'

'He thinks she accidentally fell out of a window?'

'It's a bit odd, isn't it? Perhaps it's because he pushed her himself. Anyway, Stanton supposedly has an alibi for the time of his wife's death. I don't think you're quite going to believe who it is.'

'Who?'

'Walter Ferguson.'

Augusta groaned. 'That man gets everywhere! He's awful. Tell Joyce that he can't believe a single word Ferguson says.'

'I'll let him know he can be unreliable.'

'Unreliable? That's an enormous understatement, Philip. Tell Joyce he can't accept Walter Ferguson's alibi. The man is a snake.'

'I agree with you. But it's possible he's telling the truth.'

'I don't believe he's telling the truth. He's manipulating things again. Did he know Robert Stanton before he read about the long-lost letter in the *Daily London News*?'

'I don't know.'

'I'm sure he didn't. I think he must have contacted the Stantons because he wants to investigate Alexander Miller's disappearance himself! He congratulated me for finding the letter. It wasn't sincere, of course. But I think he was envious I uncovered the case. He's trying to undermine me!'

'We can't be certain about any of this, Augusta.'

'But why else would he have got involved with the Stantons?'

'It's difficult to say. Let's see how Joyce gets on with establishing the alibi with him.'

Chapter 45

'Oh hello, Walter,' said Robert when he answered the knock at his door that evening.

'I thought I'd come and see how you're holding up, Robert.'

'I'm not sure I am, really.' He ran a hand across his brow. He wasn't in the mood for conversation. But Walter Ferguson was standing on his doorstep expecting to be invited in. Robert reasoned he would be a distraction. 'Come on in.' He stepped to one side to make room for him.

'How did you get on with the police?' Walter asked as Robert showed him to the sitting room.

'One of them looked no older than twelve.'

'Detective Sergeant Joyce from the Yard? I know who you mean.'

'I told them Jane's death was an accident.' Robert poured out two whiskies. 'But they seem to think she was pushed.'

'Do they think you did it?'

Robert handed a glass to Walter. 'Probably.'

Walter shook his head. 'It's always the way. They pick on the easiest person. The grieving husband.'

'But I was with you at the time.'

'Yes, I'll be happy to tell them that, Robert.'

'Thank you, Walter. We met at eight that evening, didn't we?'

'I think it was a little later than that.'

'Only slightly. You'll tell them eight won't you? It would help enormously. At the moment, it's not looking good for me.' He sank into his armchair. 'Can you believe they tried to suggest I had something to do with my brother-in-law's disappearance?'

'Really?'

'Quite ridiculous. Something about some money which Jane apparently owed Alexander. But the trouble is, he moaned to a friend about it who then wrote to his sister about it. And now the police seem to think Jane had an enormous debt which could only be solved if she got rid of her brother. And they seem to think I could have been in on it as well. Quite ridiculous.'

'Completely ridiculous! I remember you telling me all about the letters Mrs Peel got hold of. Don't tell me she mentioned the debt to the police?'

'She must have done.'

'That woman is nothing but trouble,' said Walter. 'She's incapable of minding her own business. She seems to think there's a mystery in everything and that everyone is up to no good. Who does she think she is?'

'If she hadn't found those letters, then I wouldn't be being questioned about the money.'

'Exactly. She's responsible for all of this! If that letter from John Gibson to his sister had been discarded ten years ago, none of this would be happening. But instead, it was left in a book which happened to land in Mrs Peel's hands.

An ordinary person would have thrown that letter into the wastepaper basket. But not Mrs Peel. No. Instead, she marched off to the woman the letter had been sent to. And then she began harassing your wife. Your poor dear, departed wife who must have had a terrible time of it. She tried to do the same to me, you know. When my colleague was murdered, she ambushed me outside my office. Quite unbelievable behaviour. And who is she, anyway? Just a woman who repairs old books and flogs them for a bit of money. Books which are so worn and tired they should just be thrown out. Somehow, she manages to make a business out of it. And, at the same time, she fancies herself as a private detective. Do you know she worked for British intelligence during the war?'

'No.' This information made him feel even warier now. 'That's very interesting to hear, Walter.'

'She needs to be brought down a peg or two. In fact, she just needs to stop doing what she's doing. I've already published a couple of articles about her in the *London Weekly Chronicle*. But my next one is going to be the best yet. In it, I'm going to be revealing her real name and where she's really from. I can tell she's worrying about it.'

'Really?'

'What I've discovered is quite astounding. You'll struggle to believe it yourself, Robert.' He grinned.

'She's a lady with a past?'

'Oh yes. And it's some past, I can tell you. Augusta Peel isn't her real name. And there's a very good reason why she keeps that secret. It's so sensational that my editor's even worrying about publishing it.'

'You must tell me more, Walter.'

'I never reveal the details of a story before it's published. This one has been slightly delayed because my editor is nervous about it. But I'm putting his mind at ease and I expect it will be published soon. You won't hear another word from her then, Robert. I guarantee it.'

'Good.'

When Walter had first turned up on his doorstep, he had told him to go away. But Walter had persisted and now he realised how useful he could be. He was going to provide him with an alibi and he was going to silence Mrs Peel. Walter Ferguson was a very helpful chap indeed.

Chapter 46

Augusta called at the little pharmacy on Marchmont Street after she had closed the bookshop for the day. She had a headache and had run out of headache powders. After she had paid Mr Barrett, the pharmacist, she noticed bottles of blood purifier on the shelves.

'What does blood purifier do?' she asked.

'Some say it helps with ulcers,' he replied. 'Along with eczema, boils and pimples.'

'Would it help someone cycle faster?'

A smile played on his lips. 'I've not heard of that.'

'I once heard of someone saying Jackson's Blood Purifier helped him cycle faster.'

'Jackson's Blood Purifier? I don't think that would have helped anyone cycle faster. It's not available anymore. It was taken off the shelves after Jackson's court case.'

'What court case was that?'

'Dr Jackson. Have you not heard about him?'

'No. When was the court case?'

'About eight or nine years ago. He wasn't a proper doctor, he'd been pretending. His blood purifier was very popular for a while, but when it was examined by the British Medical Association, it was found to be little more than water, sugar and alcohol.'

'Oh dear. So Dr Jackson went on trial?'

'No. Not for that. It was one of the countless secret remedies about at the time. Dr Jackson got into trouble for poisoning someone with a new remedy he was developing.'

'Someone died?'

'No. No one died. But a man fell unwell after being given a large dose of cocaine. Dr Jackson was investigated, and it was found he'd never qualified as a doctor and had no medical knowledge whatsoever.'

'What happened to him?'

'He went to prison, but I can't tell you how long for.'

'Interesting. So Jackson's Blood Purifier was useless?'

'Yes. I'm not sure the ones on the shelf behind me are much better these days, but all medicines are properly monitored now. The British Medical Association clamped down on all those obscure remedies before the war.'

'Thank you. That's very interesting, Mr Barrett.'

'Don't forget your headache powders, Mrs Peel.'

'Thank you. I almost did!'

Augusta was deep in thought as she returned to her flat with Sparky. Why had Alexander Miller thought the blood purifier helped him when it had probably had no effect whatsoever? It was no wonder John Gibson hadn't been helped by it at all.

She placed Sparky's cage on the dining table and opened it so he could flutter about. Then she stepped over to the window and opened it a crack so some air could get in, but Sparky couldn't get out.

A man in a dark suit was standing in the street, looking up at her window. As soon as she saw him, he looked away.

'That's him!' she said to Sparky. 'The intruder!'

Augusta left her flat and ran down the stairs. She planned to confront the man and ask him who he worked for.

As soon as she stepped out onto the street, he walked away at a brisk pace. 'Excuse me!' she called after him. 'I want a word!'

He began to run, so Augusta followed. At the top of Marchmont Street, he turned right into Compton Street again. And when he turned left by the hospital into Judd Street, Augusta guessed he was taking the same route as before. She did her best to keep up, knowing she was going to tire very soon. All she had to do was maintain her pace until they reached King's Cross station.

The man turned right into Euston Road, then dashed across it towards the underground entrance of King's Cross. Augusta did the same and felt pleased she was keeping pace with him a little better this time. Once again, the man dashed down the steps of the underground station. The ticket hall was busy again, but Augusta decided she had no time to be polite in the ticket office queue. She dashed to the front of it.

'Do you mind?' said a man with a neat beard.

'I apologise, but this is an emergency.' She swiftly got hold of a ticket, waved it at the ticket inspector, then headed for the escalator leading down to the platforms.

The fugitive was at the foot of the escalator and turning left towards the Piccadilly Line. Augusta ran down the escalator after him. The tiled corridor on the left was busy. A man bumped into her. 'Oh goodness, I'm sorry. Are you alright?'

'Yes, I'm fine, thank you,' said Augusta. She rushed on, trying to catch sight of the man she was following. It was hard to spot him in the crowd.

The corridor eventually opened out onto a platform.

The fugitive had turned right and was making his way along the platform. It was busy and a dank wind blew from the rail tunnel.

The fugitive didn't stop on the platform. Instead he continued to an exit at the far end. Augusta followed. A flight of steps led upwards, and the man took them two at a time before turning right at the top.

Augusta was tiring. He was leading her on a wild chase around the underground station and she was running out of energy to keep up.

She turned right at the top of the steps, and she was met with an empty corridor. Having just been among crowds, there was something eerie about the quiet. Where had the man gone? She walked on and reached another empty corridor which led to the right. She paused, catching her breath and listening to the distant rumble of a tube train approaching the station.

She was tired, and the man had got away. She had no urge to continue searching the station for him. She vowed to herself she would find out who he was sooner or later. She turned and made her way back to the staircase which led to the platform.

A train had arrived and she could hear its doors opening. She was just about to take the first step down when she felt a sharp shove in the small of her back.

There was nothing she could do to stop herself as she tumbled forwards down the steep, tiled steps.

Chapter 47

'WILL I be able to leave soon?' asked Augusta as the nurse tucked in her bed sheets the following day. Plump white pillows supported her aching head. The hospital bed was comfortable, but Augusta didn't want to waste her time lying there.

'Not for a while, Mrs Peel,' said the nurse. 'You've got concussion and suspected broken ribs.'

'They don't feel broken,' said Augusta, trying not to wince at the pain when she breathed. 'I'm sure it's just bruising.'

'Well, I'm afraid you can't go anywhere, Mrs Peel, until the doctor is happy for you to leave us. In the meantime, please get some rest. It will be visiting hours shortly, that will be something to look forward to.'

The sun streamed through the tall ward windows of the Middlesex Hospital. An elderly woman in the bed opposite kept grumbling about pain in her back. The lady in the bed next to her coughed every few minutes. Augusta felt irritable and grumpy.

Someone had found her at the foot of the steps near

the northbound Piccadilly Line in King's Cross underground station. She didn't know who had found her because she had been unconscious at the time. No one had seen who had pushed her.

That afternoon, Philip arrived with Fred who pushed Lady Hereford in her bath chair. Lady Hereford clutched a large bouquet of flowers and a bowl of fruit.

'Goodness me, Augusta, you look exhausted,' said Lady Hereford.

'I'm fine.'

'You can't be fine, Augusta. They don't keep people in hospital for no reason.'

'I suspect you're putting on a brave face,' said Philip.

'It's not a brave face, it's just an impatient face. I want to get back to my shop. I'm not used to lying about here. I'm taking up a bed which could be used for someone in greater need than me.'

'Well, I think the hospital knows best,' said Fred. 'They wouldn't keep you here if they didn't have to.'

'That's right,' said Lady Hereford. 'They need to keep an eye on you. You've had a nasty fall.' She turned to Philip. 'Have your lot caught the man yet, Mr Fisher?'

'Not yet. But they're working on it.'

'Why did he do this?' asked Lady Hereford.

'I think it was the same man who took the letters from my flat,' said Augusta. 'Someone must have asked him to do it. I saw him again outside my flat and I wanted to speak to him.'

'You should have called the police,' said Lady Hereford. 'You can't take matters into your own hands.'

'I just wanted to find out who he was and who he was working for.'

'You're not going to try that again, are you?' said Lady Hereford. 'You've got these two fine young men to call upon next time.'

'I thought it would be straightforward.'

She felt a wave of nausea wash over her. A pain throbbed in the left side of her chest, and she realised perhaps she should rest after all.

'Don't you worry about anything, Augusta,' said Fred, as if reading her mind. 'We can look after everything for you until you've recovered. Including Sparky. He's been quite happy at my home, and he enjoyed meeting my mother.'

'Thank you, Fred. That's very kind of you. There's something I want to look into. If you get a chance, please can you look up the trial of Dr Jackson? It was about ten years ago.'

'Of course.'

'Augusta...' warned Lady Hereford. 'You're not to discuss your detective work while lying unwell in a hospital bed.'

'Alright then. I'll get some rest now.'

'Please do. The sooner you rest, the sooner you'll be out of here again.'

Chapter 48

ROBERT STANTON FOLDED his arms and jutted his jaw at Detective Sergeant Joyce and Inspector Whitman.

'I've just been widowed,' he said. 'And you're treating me like a criminal.'

'We have a few more questions to ask,' said the inspector. 'We've spoken with your friend Walter Ferguson and the conversation raised something which we need to clarify with you. This won't take long.'

Robert sighed. 'Jane's death was an accident. There's nothing more to tell you.'

'Walter Ferguson has confirmed the pair of you met for a drink in the Westmoreland Arms public house on the evening of your wife's death,' said Detective Sergeant Joyce.

'Good.'

'You told us you met at eight o'clock.'

'That's right.'

'Mr Ferguson told us you met at nine o'clock.'

Robert's heart sank but he tried to show no reaction. What was Walter doing? He had agreed to be his alibi!

'So, can you tell me which time is correct, Mr Stanton?'

'Eight o'clock.'

'So it's your word against his, then. You say eight and he says nine. Some people would suggest I'm being petty and could let this pass. However, it's impossible to do so because your wife fell from your apartment at half-past eight. So if you met Mr Ferguson at eight o'clock, then you're in the clear. If you met him at nine o'clock, then your time is unaccounted for at the time of your wife's death.'

Robert smiled, attempting to ease the tension in the room. 'I can see what this looks like, Detective. But this is just a misunderstanding between Mr Ferguson and me. I'm adamant that we arranged to meet at eight o'clock. I got there for eight, and I think he was a little late.'

'An entire hour late?'

'No, not that long. But enough that I suppose he has it in his mind that we met at nine. That's the only thing I can think of. I can't think how else to explain why he says one time and I say the other.'

He didn't like the way the detective held his gaze. But he smiled again, hoping it would show what an amiable chap he was.

'Let's assume for a moment that it was closer to nine o'clock when you met Mr Ferguson,' said Detective Sergeant Joyce. 'Is there anyone else who can provide you with an alibi before nine o'clock that evening?'

'No.'

'So you have no alibi for the time of your wife's death. Don't you agree that looks rather suspicious, Mr Stanton?'

'It may look suspicious, but it isn't. Just because my friend refuses to provide me with an alibi from eight o'clock onwards that evening doesn't mean that it's suspicious. I was in the pub with Walter Ferguson. I got there before him, and he came along a little later. But I had nothing to do with my wife's death. It was an accident. How many times do I need to say that?'

The detective stroked his hairless chin. 'I'm sure you can appreciate that our discussion with Walter Ferguson has given us a new understanding of your whereabouts that evening, Mr Stanton. I'm afraid if you can't prove where you were at half-past eight that evening, then you will remain our main suspect.'

'I was in the Westmoreland Arms!' Robert shook his head and tried to remain calm. 'This is ridiculous.'

He had trusted Walter, but the man had let him down. It wouldn't have been difficult to tell the police eight instead of nine. The man was clearly scared of lying to them.

'Were you in the vicinity of King's Cross station yesterday, Mr Stanton?'

'No. Why?'

'A lady was injured there.'

'What happened?'

'Someone attacked her, and she's currently in hospital.'

'That's very sad, but it's nothing to do with me.'

'Are you sure? I believe you know her.'

'Tell me who she is then.'

'Mrs Peel.'

'As I've said. It was nothing to do with me.' He kept his face as straight as possible, but inwardly he felt joyful.

Augusta Peel had finally been subdued.

Chapter 49

AUGUSTA FELT a little better the following day when Philip visited. He brought her a box of Peek Freans chocolate biscuits.

'How are you feeling, Augusta?'

'Bored.'

'That must be a sign you're getting better.' Philip sat down, opened the box of biscuits and offered her one. Then he took one for himself.

'How have you been, Philip?'

'Apart from worrying about you?'

'You've been worrying about me?'

'Of course I have, Augusta! I'm furious someone has got away with pushing you down a flight of steps and injuring you like this. And it frustrates me that we can't find who did it.'

'All we need to do is find out who's behind Alexander Miller's disappearance. Then we'll know who did it. Someone's been watching me, and I suspect it's because I'm getting closer to the truth. They're the person who's scared. Not me.'

'I agree with you, Augusta. But at the present time, you're the one lying in a hospital bed. It's difficult seeing you like this.'

'But I'm getting better. I should be out of here tomorrow.'

'Even if you are, you need to take things carefully.'

'I will. Anyway. You haven't told me how you've been.'

'Ah yes.' He offered her another biscuit and took another one for himself. 'I told Mr Ramsden I could no longer work for him. He wasn't that impressed. He said it was my fault his wife spotted me among the tea towels in the department store. He told me I'd been clumsy, and I suppose there's some truth in that.'

'I don't think there's any truth in that at all! Doesn't he realise how difficult it is to follow someone around without them noticing you?'

'Clearly, he doesn't. I wish now I'd just let that thief run off with Mrs Ramsden's handbag.'

'But you're not that sort of person, Philip. You wouldn't have forgiven yourself if you'd allowed him to get away with it. It was unfortunate the incident drew Mrs Ramsden's attention to you, but it couldn't be helped. It's not clumsiness on your part or any lack of professionalism. It's just one of those things. You did what you could, and I think you've made the right decision to stop working for him.'

'I suppose so. And there is no shortage of private detectives in London, so he'll soon find someone else to do the work for him. And I told him I was quite convinced his wife wasn't having an extramarital affair. He told me I must be mistaken.'

'If he knows best, then it's just as well you're no longer working for him. It's a shame he didn't react well, but that's not your fault.'

'Well said, Augusta. Another biscuit?'

'No, I'm alright, thank you.' The pain in her rib was bothering her again, but she didn't want to admit it.

'I need one if that's alright. There's something else I need to tell you, Augusta. I wanted to wait until you were out of hospital, but I think you'd be annoyed at me for not telling you sooner.'

'Yes, I would be. What is it?'

'I visited Mr Baker at the *London Weekly Chronicle* again today. I wanted him to promise he won't be printing the article about you.'

'And?'

'It's not good news, I'm afraid, Augusta. He told me he's publishing it this Wednesday.'

'Oh no.' Augusta rested her head back against her pillow.

'I tried to do what I could. But I'm afraid it's another thing I've failed at, Augusta.'

'Oh Philip, you've not failed.' She reached out her hand and he held it. 'You did all you could. Thank you for trying. I appreciate it.'

Chapter 50

AUGUSTA WAS RELIEVED to finally leave hospital and get back to her bookshop. Sparky seemed happy to see her again and even treated her to a song. The pain in her ribs was improving, but she was careful not to do too much to avoid a scolding from Philip and Fred.

Mr Ramsden called in at her shop on her first day back. Clearly, he was still keen to buy her books, even though Philip was no longer working for him.

'It's a pleasure to see you here again, Mr Ramsden,' she said.

'That's because I can't go without my weekly visit to your delightful shop, Mrs Peel. I'm a quick reader and so here I am, back for more.' He smiled. 'Although I shan't be paying a visit to your friend, Mr Fisher, today. He's no longer working for me.'

Augusta feigned ignorance. 'Is he not?'

'No. Unfortunately, he's attracted the attentions of my wife. She always responds well to a handsome face. And that's the mistake I made in choosing Mr Fisher, I think. I should have perhaps found someone who is less likely to catch her attention. A woman, perhaps? Now there's a thought. Mr Fisher mentioned to me that you do a bit of sleuthing yourself, Mrs Peel. I don't suppose you'd be interested in the work, would you?'

'Oh.' Augusta hadn't expected the question. 'What sort of work, Mr Ramsden?'

'Gathering evidence on my wife's infidelity.'

She made her excuse quickly. 'I'm afraid this shop keeps me far too busy to devote any time to such a task, Mr Ramsden.'

'Well, that is a shame. Because you're the sort of lady my wife wouldn't look twice at.'

'Is that a compliment or an insult, Mr Ramsden?'

'Good grief, what a terrible thing I said! It makes me sound as though I'm describing you as completely plain and uninteresting. Nothing could be further from the truth, Mrs Peel. What I'm trying to say is you have a certain ordinariness about you. And I hope you're not offended by that. Your appearance allows you to blend in. Your clothes don't seek attention and you don't paint your face with bold colours. My wife, being the sort of lady she is, would probably stroll past you without realising you were following her. That said, I can tell it isn't a job you particularly wish to take on. So I shall cease discussion of it and browse the shelves of your shop, if I may?'

'Of course, Mr Ramsden.'

After Mr Ramsden had bought three books, Fred told Augusta what he had learned about Dr Jackson from reading about his trial in old newspapers at the library.

'He told people his name was Dr Herbert Jackson. He'd been an army doctor in India and, during his time there, he'd learned about traditional preparations which

Indian people used to treat various ailments. On his return to Britain, he decided to use this knowledge to make and sell preparations of his own. He left the army and created Jackson's Blood Purifier. It sold well, and he set up a small laboratory and factory in Finchley.'

'Finchley?'

'Yes.'

'Where the Connolly family lives. Sorry to interrupt you Fred, please continue.'

'He also rented a room on Harley Street to give himself and his product a more exclusive reputation. The medicine was quite expensive, but the high price reassured people it was good quality. Dr Jackson advertised to people who could afford this price, including the readers of *Aristo* magazine. He also extolled its health benefits to people who liked to exercise, such as the readers of the *Cycling Club Magazine*.'

'Which must be how Alexander Miller learned about it!' said Augusta.

'Miller took the remedy?'

'Yes. He told John Gibson that it made him cycle faster.'

'So this is why you asked me to look into Dr Jackson.'

'Yes. We have a connection with Miller and Finchley now. Please continue, Fred.'

'Once Jackson's Blood Purifier was an established success, Dr Herbert Jackson began work on a new remedy. It was described as a health boosting remedy to help people live healthier, longer lives. And this is where Dr Jackson got into trouble. He paid people to try out the new remedy and accidentally poisoned one of them.'

'Was the person named in the trial?'

'Yes, Stephen Allen. He fell unwell after leaving Dr

Jackson's laboratory and collapsed in the street. He was taken to hospital and Dr Jackson's new remedy was examined. It was found to contain cocaine, and a large dose had been administered to Mr Allen. When the British Medical Association investigated, it discovered Dr Jackson wasn't a doctor at all. His name was Daniel Collins, and he had never been an army doctor. Nor had he ever travelled to India. He was fifty-eight years old, lived in Finchley, and had worked as a travelling salesman for a soap company before inventing his blood purifier.'

'What a scoundrel!'

'Jackson's Blood Purifier was removed from sale and the medicine was examined by the British Medical Association,' said Fred. 'It wasn't as dangerous as the remedy which had poisoned people. It was found to contain alcohol, water and sugar.'

'Which is what the pharmacist on my street told me,' said Augusta. 'So Dr Jackson charged people a high price for something which was completely ineffective. What happened to him?'

'He stood trial in 1912 for the poisoning. The judge found Mr Collins hadn't intentionally poisoned Mr Allen, he'd only done so because he'd been ignorant about the effects of cocaine. The judge was critical of the fact Collins had pretended to be a doctor when he had no medical qualifications. Despite everything, the judge actually praised his salesmanship and told him he should have remained working for the soap company.'

'What was his sentence?'

'Five years.'

'So he went to prison and lost his lucrative business.'

'Yes. What does this have to do with Alexander Miller?'

'I'm not sure yet. But he used Jackson's Blood Purifier and swore that it helped him cycle faster. And his accident with Mr Connolly took place in Finchley. So we know he visited the place.'

'Perhaps it's more a coincidence?'

Perhaps it could be. But maybe it isn't and he knew Dr Jackson? Or Daniel Collins, to give him his real name.'

Chapter 51

'JACKSON'S BLOOD PURIFIER AND FINCHLEY,' said Augusta once she had explained the latest development to Philip. 'That's what Dr Jackson and Alexander Miller have in common.'

'You think they knew each other?'

'It's possible.'

They sat in Philip's office drinking tea. Augusta got up from her chair, walked over to the blackboard and wrote Dr Jackson's name on it. 'His real name is Daniel Collins,' she said as she added the second name. 'We know he tested a new remedy on a man called Stephen Allen. Mr Allen fell unwell and was admitted to hospital. It was found he'd suffered an overdose of cocaine.' She turned to Philip. 'What if there were more Mr Allens?'

'More people who Dr Jackson tested his remedy on? There must have been.'

'Perhaps Alexander Miller was one of them.'

'He could have been. He took the blood purifier, and we know he was in Finchley at least once. But only Mr Allen was poisoned.'

'He's the only one we know about. But maybe there were others?'

'Then we'd know about them too.'

'Not if they didn't survive.'

'You think someone could have been fatally poisoned by Dr Jackson?'

Augusta nodded.

'Alexander Miller?'

'Yes. And Dr Jackson was so horrified about what happened that he covered up the death.'

'That would take some covering up.'

'It could have happened at his Finchley laboratory. There may have been no one else around at the time.'

'But he would've had to dispose of Miller, too, without anyone finding out. It's an interesting idea, Augusta. But I've no idea how you prove it.'

'Me neither.' She returned to her chair and sat down. 'I feel quite puzzled by this. I feel like I'm getting close to the answer, but... it's evading me. And it doesn't help that Walter Ferguson's article is being printed tomorrow.'

'Ah yes.' Philip took a sip of tea. 'That is unfortunate.'

'It's more than unfortunate! It's... oh, I don't want to dwell on it! Ferguson wants me to worry about it and so I refuse to do so.'

Philip put down his cup and saucer. 'You know who would be extremely useful in this case, don't you, Augusta?'

'Who?'

Philip got up from his chair and went over to the little shelf with one book on it.

'I know what you're going to say,' said Augusta. 'Sherlock Holmes.'

'That's right.' He picked up *The Adventures of Sherlock Holmes*. 'He lived on Baker Street, didn't he? If only we could call on him. I can picture myself standing in Baker

Street at night, looking up at the light glowing from his window. And there his silhouette passes across the blind as he paces back and forth, contemplating his latest case.'

Augusta smiled. 'Very poetic, Philip. Unfortunately he's fictional.'

'And more's the pity. But perhaps we can think like him, Augusta.'

'I don't think anybody can think like Sherlock Holmes. Isn't that why he was considered to be so brilliant?'

'True. He was outwitted once, wasn't he? By the singer and actress, Irene Adler. It's in one of these stories.' He leafed through the book. '*A Scandal in Bohemia*. That's the one.'

'Much as I wish Sherlock Holmes could help us, he can't,' said Augusta. 'So we have to come up with some ideas ourselves.'

Chapter 52

Augusta woke before dawn and lay awake for some time, angry with herself for allowing Walter Ferguson to upset her this much. She tried to tell herself it didn't matter. But it did. And that was why she felt upset. The very last thing she wanted was someone in her family seeing the article. For years, she had been able to live her life as she chose. The war, although difficult, had opened her eyes to a range of experiences. Some had been good, and others bad. But they had all fashioned her into the person she was now.

Some memories from the war haunted her still. But being able to live a life she had chosen for herself had given her a great deal of contentment. It didn't matter that she hadn't been born Augusta Peel. She was Augusta Peel now.

Once people learned about her past, they would treat her differently. It would change everything. This quiet life of contentment was about to come to an end.

. . .

The newsagent on Marchmont Street opened at six o'clock. Augusta washed, dressed, gave Sparky an early breakfast, and made her way there for opening time. Reluctantly, she bought a copy of the *London Weekly Chronicle*. Then she walked back to her flat. Her knees felt weak and her feet felt disconnected from the ground. As if she were floating. It was an uncomfortable sensation. She felt present and absent at the same time.

The tailor's wife greeted her and she smiled a good morning. She climbed the stairs to her flat and her limbs felt numb. Once inside the flat, she locked all three locks on her door. She wanted to keep the world out.

The tailor's wife had greeted her happily, but she was going to discover who Augusta really was. After that she would treat her differently. Just like everyone else.

Walter Ferguson was about to change everything in her life.

Augusta placed the newspaper on the dining table and sat down. Sparky fluttered about the room as she ran her eyes over the front page. There was no mention of her there. Her heart thudded and her hands trembled as she turned over the first page. She felt nauseous as her eyes bounced over each headline, searching out for mention of her name or a lady spy or bookseller.

She turned the next page.

And then the next.

After turning a few more pages, Augusta felt reassured. The editor was giving the article little prominence. Hopefully this would mean fewer people would see it.

She turned another page. And then another. There was still no sign of the article. Had she missed it? Confused, she turned back to the beginning of the newspaper again.

Perhaps the article had been so obvious that she had simply overlooked it.

But no, she couldn't see it. She turned back to the middle of the newspaper and continued on. The pages were now showing sporting results and classified advertisements. She turned the page again and again, and her heart rate began to slow a little when she reached the back page.

There was no mention of her. But she didn't want to breathe a sigh of relief just yet. Surely, she had missed something. She turned back to the first page of the newspaper and began again.

Chapter 53

'Perhaps I'm not looking properly,' Augusta said to Fred when she arrived at the bookshop with Sparky. 'But I can't find the article which Walter Ferguson claims to have written about me.' She handed him the copy of the newspaper. 'Can you see it in here?'

'Perhaps it hasn't been published after all?' said Fred.

'I doubt that. Walter Ferguson has been talking about it for weeks and the editor told Philip that he intended to publish it.'

'I'll have a look for you,' said Fred. 'But I can't imagine you're mistaken.'

'I probably am. I've got myself into such a state about this. I woke up early worrying about it. I'm worried now that I can't think straight.'

'Let's see,' said Fred. He laid the newspaper on the counter and began to leaf through it. Augusta distracted herself by feeding some birdseed to Sparky. As Fred turned each page, she grew increasingly hopeful the article hadn't been printed after all.

Finally he reached the end. 'I can't see it,' he said. 'You weren't imagining it, Augusta. It hasn't been printed.'

Augusta blew out a sigh of relief. 'Thank goodness. But what does this mean? Perhaps they're going to print it next week instead?'

She turned as she heard footsteps on the stairs and Philip appeared.

'Good morning!' His greeting was cheerful.

'Good morning, Philip. Fred and I can't find the article in the *London Weekly Chronicle*.'

'That's because it hasn't been published.'

'We've realised that. Have you looked through the paper already?'

'No. I managed to talk some sense into a junior minister at the War Office late yesterday. I went down there in person and refused to leave until I could speak to someone important there. I explained to the minister what the editor of the *London Weekly Chronicle* was planning to do and told him the War Office needs to have a firm word with the editor and instruct him not to publish. The minister was concerned and said he'd do what he could. Thankfully, it looks like he's succeeded.'

'Thank you, Philip!' Augusta couldn't help herself. She stepped over to him and embraced him. 'I'm so happy you persuaded them!'

She stepped back again and Philip looked a little embarrassed as he straightened his tie.

'I merely explained to the minister that the War Office needed to read the article to find out what information was illicitly passed to Walter Ferguson. If he was given details which could only have been obtained from your file, Augusta, then he has a case to answer to. As does the person in the War Office who gave him that information.'

'I hope they get into trouble for it,' said Augusta.

'It hasn't put a complete stop to Ferguson,' said Philip. 'Maybe he'll try to print a modified version of his article. But that can't contain anything which isn't already publicly known. So I think your secrets are safe for now, Augusta.'

Chapter 54

WALTER FERGUSON MARCHED into Mr Baker's office. He didn't bother to knock. The editor startled and got to his feet.

'What happened?' said Walter. He could feel himself shaking with rage.

Mr Baker was a bald, feeble looking man. Walter felt sure he could fell him with just one blow. 'The government got involved, that's what happened,' said the editor.

'The *government*? How?'

'I received a telephone call yesterday from a junior minister at the War Office. He requested to see the article about Mrs Peel because he was concerned it contained illegally obtained information.'

'And how did he know about it?'

'I don't know. Perhaps Mrs Peel mentioned it to him.'

'Does she know him?'

'I don't know, Mr Ferguson. Anyway, with a request like that, I had to speak to the proprietor of this newspaper, Mr Granger. He was alarmed to hear the War Office was concerned about the article. He told me to comply with their request, so I did.'

'Ridiculous!'

'Concern had been expressed that confidential information had been obtained from files held within the War Office. What sources did you use for your article, Mr Ferguson?'

'My usual sources. As I've told you before, I know people who know Mrs Peel.'

'And I don't expect you to name them. However, if they have given you information which is supposed to remain confidential, it shouldn't be made public. No matter how well you know this person or people. Anyway, the long and the short of it was the minister decided there was information in the article which could not be used because it could only have been obtained from War Office files. So, he upheld the complaint that was put to him and he informed me that we wouldn't be able to publish at all.'

Walter sank down into a chair. All the air had left him. He shook his head in dismay. 'Mrs Peel has pulled strings yet again. I didn't realise she was so well acquainted with figures in the government. That woman is beyond belief.'

'Your article revealed her true identity, Mr Ferguson. If you can prove you found that information from somewhere other than the files held on Mrs Peel at the War Office, then we have a good argument for proceeding with publication. But if you sourced it illegally, then I'm afraid our hands are tied. We have an official order from the War Office that we are unable to print the article. If you think you can prove you obtained the information legitimately, then we can proceed. It really is up to you, Mr Ferguson.'

'Up to me? But you're the editor of this newspaper! You should be arguing my case!'

'And I have done my best to do so. But without

knowing exactly where you got that information, I can't convince the minister that the article should be published.'

Walter put his head in his hands. Mrs Peel had won again. The ordinary bookseller who had worked as a spy in the war. She was such a plain-looking woman that you could walk past her in the street without giving her a second glance. And yet she always managed to succeed.

'It was a very interesting article, Mr Ferguson,' said the editor. 'The secret history of the spy-turned-bookseller intrigues us all.'

Walter set back in his chair. He had done so much work on this. He had even paid the War Office archives clerk out of his own pocket. But his efforts had been for nothing. He imagined how Mrs Peel would be feeling today. Relieved and happy that the article he had threatened her with would no longer appear.

All he could do now was solve the disappearance of Alexander Miller. He had befriended Miller's brother-in-law and gained his confidence. He had also read all of John Gibson's letters. The case was almost solved! The editor, proprietor and Scotland Yard were going to be eternally grateful to him.

After leaving the editor's office, Walter went downstairs and stepped out onto Fleet Street. He needed some air. Even if it wasn't particularly clean air.

The sun was shining, and he enjoyed the warmth on his face. He was going to solve the case of Alexander Miller. And he couldn't wait for Augusta Peel to read about it in the newspaper. She was going to be very upset about him solving it before her.

'Walter!' came a shout from behind him.

He turned to see the angry, square face of Robert Stanton. 'Hello, Robert. What a surprise.'

'I thought we agreed you'd provide me with an alibi.'

'We did. And I did.'

'No, you didn't. You told the police we met at nine.'

'Because we did.'

'I told you to say eight.'

'Did you?'

'You told me you'd help me!'

'I did and I am! I think there must have been a misunder—'

Walter didn't finish his sentence because the blow from Robert's fist sent him crashing to the ground.

Chapter 55

AFTER CLOSING the shop for the day, Augusta went up the stairs to Philip's office. She was pleased to find he hadn't yet left for home.

'I never thought I'd say this,' she said. 'But I think Sherlock Holmes can help with this case after all.'

'Even though he's a fictional detective, Augusta? You reminded me of that when I mentioned him.'

'Yes, even though he's a fictional detective. I think there's a story which could apply to our case. Can I have a look at *The Adventures of Sherlock Holmes*?'

'By all means. Are you sure you'll be able to find it on my shelf?'

Augusta smiled and picked up the book. 'I recall there's a story with a typewriter,' she said. 'And I remember it's a young woman who asks for Sherlock Holmes's help.' She continued to flick through the pages. 'I think it might be this one. *A Case of Identity*.'

'Oh yes, that one.'

'Are you thinking what I'm thinking, Philip?'

'I doubt it. You're going to have to explain a bit more, Augusta.'

'I need to do some research tomorrow,' she said, putting the book back on the shelf. 'And then I'm going to visit Jemima Campbell. After that, I might just have a plan.'

Chapter 56

AUGUSTA VISITED Holborn Library in the morning and then the public records offices in Somerset House. Then she called on Constable Simpson at Crawford Place police station before travelling by train to Wimbledon. A theory was developing in her mind. But was she on the right track? She hoped Jemima Campbell would be able to help.

It was late morning when Augusta rang the doorbell at the neat semi-detached house. A scent of jasmine lingered in the well-tended front garden.

'Oh.' There was no smile from Mrs Campbell when she opened the door. She kept a hand on the latch as if intending to close the door again shortly.

Augusta was reminded of the lacklustre response from Mrs Bradshaw's housekeeper. Had Mrs Campbell also been threatened? Augusta couldn't allow the door to be closed on her again. She prepared herself to put a foot in the way if necessary.

'Mrs Campbell, it's obvious you don't wish to speak to me. Perhaps someone has warned you not to?'

'I'm afraid I'm busy.'

'It's really important that I speak with you. I think I'm close to finding out what happened to Alexander Miller.'

The door began to close a little and Augusta got her foot ready.

'Does Dr Jackson mean anything to you?'

The flicker of fear in Jemima's expression was unmistakable.

'If you don't want to tell me anything now, then that's fine. But you clearly know something, and I suspect it's a secret you've been hiding for many years.'

Augusta noticed Jemima's eyes dampen.

'People have been threatened,' she continued. 'It's completely understandable that you're frightened. I have a very good friend who knows a lot of people in the Metropolitan Police.'

'No, I can't speak to the police!' The door closed a little more.

'He can guarantee your safety,' said Augusta. 'And the safety of your family, too. Please trust me. This can't go on any longer. People are frightened and more than one person has lost their life. Let's put an end to this now, Mrs Campbell. With your help, we can do this.'

Augusta held her breath during the silence which followed.

To her relief, the door opened a little. A tear ran down Mrs Campbell's cheek. She swiftly wiped it away.

'Can you trust me?' Augusta asked her.

Mrs Campbell nodded.

'Good. Thank you. If you're happy to talk, then please can I use your telephone? I'll telephone my friend and he'll make sure you and your family are protected. I promise.'

Chapter 57

A FEW HOURS LATER, Augusta sat in a wood-panelled room in Scotland Yard with Jemima Campbell, Philip and Detective Sergeant Joyce. In a room close by were Mrs Campbell's husband and two children. They were accompanied by a police constable. Mrs Campbell had insisted on knowing her family was safe before agreeing to speak.

'Alexander and John cycled together every weekend.' Her hands fidgeted in her lap as she spoke. 'They adored it. John liked it because he enjoyed visiting places. Alexander liked it because he was quite competitive. He hoped to get good enough at it so he could enter races. John remarked to me one day that Alexander was faster than him because he cheated. When I asked how Alexander could possibly cheat, John told me Alexander took a daily remedy. Jackson's Blood Purifier. I told John he should take it too. He did, and it didn't make him any faster.' She smiled. 'He was quite annoyed about that.

'Then, one day, Alexander told me a bit about Dr Jackson's company. He told me his brother-in-law had put money into the company and was expecting a good return on his investment. Dr Jackson was apparently developing a new remedy which could help people get stronger. Alexander's brother-in-law had told him Dr Jackson was looking for people to test the new remedy and he would pay well.'

'Alexander's brother-in-law,' said Philip. 'Is that Robert Stanton?'

'I can't remember his name, I'm afraid.'

'Robert Stanton was married to Alexander's sister, Jane.'

'That sounds about right,' said Mrs Campbell. 'Alexander did mention his sister from time to time.'

'So, did Alexander test the new remedy?' asked Detective Sergeant Joyce.

'Yes, he did. He would cycle to Dr Jackson's laboratory in Finchley and take a dose of it and cycle home again. He told me its effects were incredible.'

Knowing the remedy had contained cocaine, Augusta wasn't surprised to hear this.

'Alexander said he got on well with the doctor,' continued Mrs Campbell. 'And the doctor was keen to test out various doses on him because he did so much cycling. The pair of them apparently worked on improving Alexander's fitness and cycling speed. He was very happy. Apart from when he had the accident on his way back from the laboratory... that was a difficult time. Especially when the family blamed him for it. But he recovered and continued his work for Dr Jackson. Eventually I was persuaded to try it too.'

'You also took the new remedy?' asked Augusta.

Mrs Campbell nodded. 'Dr Jackson paid well. Five shillings for each dose. I only went along once a month because that was what he advised. I think Alexander saw him more often. Alexander always accompanied me when I visited the laboratory. I felt more comfortable having him with me. We would take the train there together and the laboratory was only a short walk from the station.'

'What was Dr Jackson like?' asked Augusta.

Mrs Campbell paused before replying. 'He was charming but I also found him intimidating. I didn't really like him very much but he seemed to know what he was doing. He was professional and I simply did what he asked me to do. He wasn't the sort of man you would argue with.'

'What makes you say that?'

'Because I felt I didn't have a chance against him. I only got involved because I earned good money from doing what he said. I was young and foolish. I shouldn't have done it. I thought I knew best at the time.'

'Did you feel any effects from the remedy?'

Mrs Campbell nodded. 'Oh yes. It was invigorating. Its effects lasted for a couple of hours, and, during that time, it felt as though all my worries slipped away. The experience was pleasurable, and I was looking forward to it being available in pharmacies to buy. Alexander swore it was strengthening him.' She sighed. 'But when Dr Jackson went on trial, we all heard what was in that remedy. It was no wonder it had such an effect on people. I feel so ashamed now that I took it!'

'You weren't to know,' said Augusta. 'You trusted Dr Jackson.'

'And how I wish I hadn't!'

'So please tell us, Mrs Campbell,' said Joyce. 'What happened to Alexander Miller?'

Chapter 58

'ALEXANDER and I travelled to Dr Jackson's laboratory on the afternoon of Saturday 2nd July,' said Mrs Campbell. 'It was a nice sunny day and Alexander was in a good mood. Everything was perfectly normal.

'Dr Jackson greeted us in his laboratory as usual. There was nothing different about him at all. He told us he'd been working on new doses for the pair of us.'

'Were you nervous about that?' asked Augusta.

'Not really. I trusted him. Fool that I was! So I took my dose and Alexander took his.'

'They were different doses?' asked Philip.

'Yes. Dr Jackson said men could handle much larger doses than women. It made sense to me at the time. And then we were just leaving the laboratory when... that's when Alexander collapsed.'

'It was completely sudden?' Augusta asked.

'Yes. A moment before, he said something about a tightness in his chest. I was just about to respond when his legs just gave way beneath him. I knelt beside him and called his name, but...' Mrs Campbell took a breath to recover herself. 'He was drifting away.'

'What did Dr Jackson do?' asked Philip.

'He told me to calm down. I was panicking, you see. He told me to get up and stop worrying because he was a doctor. Then he tried to speak to Alexander, but he was unresponsive. I said I could telephone a doctor and he got angry with me. He told me again that he was a doctor and that I didn't need to telephone anyone. Then he told me to stop being hysterical and to go home. I didn't know what to do or say. As I've said, he wasn't the sort of person you could argue with.

'So I left the laboratory and headed for the railway station. I was in a daze. In shock, I suppose. I'd only walked about twenty yards when Dr Jackson caught up with me. He told me Alexander was coming round and was going to be alright but he needed to keep an eye on him so he was going to keep him at the laboratory for the time being. I asked if I could see him, and he told me no because Alexander's condition was still delicate.'

Mrs Campbell paused and took a breath.

Augusta reached out and rested a hand on her arm. 'I can understand why this is so difficult for you. You're doing a brilliant job of explaining it all so clearly.'

'I hope I am. And I hope you can see why I haven't been able to tell anyone about this. I was only twenty at the time, and Dr Jackson was so intimidating. He told me I wasn't to breathe a word of what had happened to anybody. I asked about Alexander's family, surely they would need to know what happened to him? He told me he would speak to them personally. He said I was to leave everything to him and I mustn't even think of taking matters into my own hands. Then he pulled some money out of his pocket. A bundle of ten-shilling notes. He gave it to me and urged me to take it. I didn't want to disobey him, so I did. He then said that if I ever breathed a word about what had happened, then he would know about it. He would come for me. And that was the last time I saw him.'

'He threatened you,' said Philip.

Mrs Campbell nodded. 'And that's when I ran. I ran to the station, desperate to get away from there. I got on a train and I went home and... I didn't know what to do with myself.

'The fear has never gone away. And back then I believed Dr Jackson when he told me Alexander was getting better. I honestly thought I would see him at work on Monday and he would be joking about what had happened. I was so naive!

'Everyone was asking where Alexander was on that Monday. No one knew he and I had visited Dr Jackson at the weekend. So I just kept quiet and assumed Alexander was recovering in hospital somewhere. After a few days, I grew quite worried about him. John had said he hadn't been able to contact him. At that point, I guessed he was in hospital and that his family knew what had happened. But as time passed with no word about Alexander, I began to doubt Dr Jackson. I suspected he had caused Alexander some serious harm, and I'd played a part in it.

'John was confused. He couldn't understand what had happened to Alexander. I didn't know what to say to him and I was worried I might accidentally give myself away. When everyone was looking for Alexander, I tried to stay out of it. I felt like I was guilty of the crime. I had seen what had happened and I had told no one about it. So I kept silent. I was convinced I would stand trial for Alexander's death if anyone ever found out what I knew.

'And then John heard Alexander had written to his

sister. Apparently, there was something strange about the letter, as if Alexander hadn't written it. But I wanted to believe it was from him. I wanted to believe he had gone off and started a new life in the north. That perhaps, after his long recovery in hospital, he had decided to begin again elsewhere. I suppose I consoled myself with that thought. I never met Alexander's sister, so I didn't know what she truly thought about it. I don't think the letter convinced John either, he thought it was mysterious. But I chose to believe it because it was easier for me. I could convince myself it was the truth, and I'd done nothing wrong.

'I blame myself for what happened because I should have told someone about it. I should never have trusted Dr Jackson to look after him. Alexander had still been alive when I left him. If a proper doctor had seen him then, perhaps he could have been saved. I can't believe how foolish I was.

'The memory of Alexander collapsing has haunted me every day. It was particularly difficult when I read the newspaper reports of Dr Jackson's trial for poisoning someone. When I discovered he hadn't been a real doctor after all, I was furious! And I felt even more ashamed of how gullible I had been.'

'Were you tempted to tell someone about Alexander when you learned about Dr Jackson's trial?' asked Philip.

'There were moments when I considered it. But by then I felt like a criminal too. I had covered up someone's death. I was much too scared to walk into a police station to tell my story. I felt sure I would go on trial too. And even though Dr Jackson received a prison sentence, I knew he would be out again one day and he'd be able to come for me if I ever told anyone what had happened. So I just got on with my life. It was selfish of me. But I married and then I had children to look after and I did all I could to forget.'

'When I called on you earlier today, Mrs Campbell, you looked frightened,' said Augusta. 'Why was that?'

'Because I heard from him again.'

'Dr Jackson?'

'The letter was anonymous.'

'You received a typewritten letter?'

'Yes. How did you know?'

'Because he likes to send typewritten letters. What did the letter say?'

'It threatened me and my family. I knew immediately that it had to be from him. And I received it after I spoke to you, Mrs Peel. Somehow, he knew you had visited me. Even all these years later.'

'Do you still have the letter?' Augusta asked.

'Yes.'

'I think Detective Sergeant Joyce needs to see it,' said Augusta.

'Me?' said Joyce.

'Yes. Along with this one.' Augusta pulled the letter from her bag which she had collected from Constable Simpson at Crawford Place police station that morning. 'This is the letter Jane Stanton received from someone claiming to be her brother.' She passed it to him. 'We also need the threatening letter which was sent to Louisa Bradshaw.'

'And the reason?' asked Joyce.

'We can find out if they were all written on the same typewriter. I suspect they were.'

'Yes, I think we can guess they were.'

'And then we find the typewriter.'

'Just like *A Case of Identity*,' said Philip with a smile.

'I don't understand,' said Joyce.

'It's a Sherlock Holmes story,' said Philip. 'And in the story, it's proven that a letter was written on a specific type-writer. This isn't just the stuff of fiction, Joyce, it's a fact that every typewriter has a style of its own. Every machine has a unique defect, whether it's misalignment or an uneven strike. These defects are often subtle, but a trained eye can spot them.'

'I don't know about subtle. Most of the typewriters here at the Yard have quite obvious defects.'

'I couldn't agree more, Joyce. And I happen to know a chap who's skilled at analysing typewriting.' Philip turned to Augusta. 'It should be easy to prove the three letters were written on the same typewriter. But what about the typewriter itself? How do we find that?'

'I have an idea,' she said. 'Let's meet at an address on Farringdon Road tomorrow morning.'

'Farringdon Road?' said Joyce.

'It's one possible location for the typewriter.'

Chapter 59

'ARE YOU SURE ABOUT THIS, AUGUSTA?' Philip surveyed the building towering over them on Farringdon Road. A cool breeze whipped along the street and a train rumbled out of Farringdon railway station behind them.

'Fairly sure.' She tried not to doubt herself. She had done her research, and she had to hope everything would go smoothly.

Detective Sergeant Joyce joined them with two police constables in tow. 'I've brought a couple of chaps with me from Clerkenwell station,' he said. 'Just in case we're onto something here.'

'I should hope we're onto something!' said Philip. 'I can't say I want to walk into this building and make a fool of myself.'

Augusta looked up at the name on the building: Hodgson. 'We are onto something,' she said. 'Let's go inside.'

Joyce told the two constables to wait outside for a signal from him and they stepped into the building.

They were kept waiting in the reception area before a clerk showed them to a plush meeting room. Five minutes later, a tall, smartly dressed, grey-haired man entered the room.

'Mr Fisher!' he said. 'And Mrs Peel! This is a surprise!'

'And I'm Detective Sergeant Joyce.'

Mr Ramsden's smile faded. 'Detective?' He turned to Philip. 'What's this about?'

'Let's take a seat, Mr Ramsden. Would you like to begin, Augusta?'

'Yes.' She took a pile of papers from her handbag and shuffled them about as she prepared herself.

'Will this be quick?' asked Mr Ramsden. 'I have an appointment shortly.'

Augusta took in a breath and began. 'Have you ever heard of Daniel Collins, Mr Ramsden?'

He blinked, but his face otherwise remained impassive. 'No.' He steepled his fingers on the table and gave her a steely look.

'Daniel Collins was jailed for five years in 1912 for mistakenly poisoning Stephen Allen.'

'How careless of him.'

'At the time of the poisoning, Mr Collins was calling himself Dr Jackson. Have you ever heard of him, Mr Ramsden?'

'No.'

'You've not heard of Jackson's Blood Purifier?'

'Oh yes, I've heard of that.'

'It was a remedy which Dr Jackson made a lot of money from. Until he poisoned someone with a new remedy he was developing.'

'By accident.'

'Of course. Have you ever heard of Alexander Miller, Mr Ramsden?'

'No. It seems I haven't heard of any of these people

you're talking about, Mrs Peel. I think you could be wasting my time.'

'Alexander Miller went missing in 1911,' said Augusta. 'At the time of his disappearance, he had been taking regular doses of Dr Jackson's newly developed remedy. It turns out Mr Allen wasn't the only person who was poisoned by Dr Jackson. Mr Miller was also poisoned by him. And, unfortunately for Mr Miller, he didn't survive.'

'Was his body ever found?'

'No.'

'So how can you say he died?'

'It's quite obvious he died. He collapsed in Dr Jackson's laboratory and was never seen again.'

'And how do you know this?'

'There was a witness, Mr Ramsden.' She noticed his jaw tighten. 'A witness who remained silent for ten years because Dr Jackson had threatened her. And she wasn't the only person Dr Jackson threatened. When news of a long-lost letter about Alexander Miller was published in a news-paper, the recipient of the letter was also threatened. Louisa Bradshaw, the sister of John Gibson. He had sent her the letter describing the disappearance of his friend.

'It seems the publication of the news about the long-lost letter spurned Dr Jackson to embark on a new campaign of intimidation. He didn't want anyone specu-lating on what could have happened to Alexander Miller. He had already got rid of someone who tried too hard to find him. And that was Miller's friend, John Gibson. Dr Jackson must have grown worried that Gibson's efforts would lead him to the truth. Dr Jackson couldn't allow that to happen because it would have ended his lucrative busi-ness. He must have wanted John Gibson silenced. That's why he was pushed beneath a train at Baker Street station.'

'How do you know it wasn't an accident?' asked Mr Ramsden.

'There was quite a debate about it at his inquest. The witnesses couldn't agree on what had happened. But I think it's most likely Gibson was pushed. Dr Jackson must have been relieved once Mr Gibson was out of the way. Unfortunately for him, he went on to poison someone else though, and the gentleman lived to tell the tale. The law caught up with Dr Jackson and he stood trial for poisoning Stephen Allen. After five years in prison, people must have assumed that was the end of him.

'By the time he left prison in 1917, Dr Jackson had probably been forgotten by most people. Britain was in the grip of war. Times had changed drastically. It was the perfect time for Dr Jackson to reinvent himself into someone new. Daniel Collins had become Dr Jackson. Then Dr Jackson became Anthony Ramsden.'

He threw his head back and gave a loud laugh. 'So this is where it's all been leading! Me?' He jabbed his thumb at his chest. 'Me? Mrs Peel? You think I was Dr Jackson?'

'And Daniel Collins. You were born in the same year.'

He laughed again. 'Oh I see. I must be him then. How do you know what year I was born in?'

'I paid a visit to Somerset House yesterday to look at some public records. Not only were you born in the same year as Daniel Collins, but you were both born in Finchley. You changed your name, but you failed to change some of the other essential details.'

'Just a coincidence, Mrs Peel.'

'You incorporated Hodgson Medicines in 1917, which was the year you left prison. And having had such success with Jackson's Blood Purifier before the war, you emulated it by creating more medicines. But this time you manufactured proper medicines. The British Medical Association brought in new regulations for medicines shortly before the war. Pharmaceutical companies now have to follow certain rules and standards. Over the past four years, you've had a lot of success with a perfectly legitimate company. You married in 1918—'

'You leave my wife out of this!'

'Your marriage certificate states you were a bachelor at the time of your marriage. It's quite unusual to be married for the first time at the age of sixty-four. And as much as I searched, I couldn't find any records for Anthony Ramsden before 1917. Not even a birth certificate.'

'How do you know when and where I was born?'

'I got that information from the records held by Companies House. Now, can you explain what happened with Jane Stanton?'

'Who?'

'She was Alexander Miller's sister. I'm sure you would have known her because Robert Stanton invested in your company.'

He frowned. 'I don't think he did.'

'Let me clarify. While you were pretending to be Dr Jackson, Mr Stanton invested in Jackson's Blood Purifier.'

'Never heard of him.'

'It will be interesting to see what Robert Stanton says about that then,' said Philip.

Mr Ramsden gave him a sharp glance. Then he stroked his chin as if deliberating whether to admit knowing the Stantons or not. It was evident he would soon look foolish when Robert Stanton told a story different from his.

'What did you do with Alexander Miller's body, Mr Ramsden?' asked Philip.

Mr Ramsden sat back, startled by the directness of the question.

'I know nothing about him.'

'You must have panicked when it happened. You paid off his young companion and threatened her not to say a word. But what did you do with Alexander's body? Perhaps you'll be kind enough to tell us his final resting place.'

Mr Ramsden said nothing.

'Then you're less of a man than I thought you were, Ramsden,' said Philip. 'To cause that suffering and still not reveal where you put him.'

'Now look here!' Mr Ramsden leant forward and jabbed his finger into the table. 'You have no evidence!'

'We're in the process of gathering it.'

'And can you assure us it's just coincidence you asked Mr Fisher to follow your wife shortly after the news of the long-lost letter was published?' said Augusta.

'Of course.'

'I don't believe you. Once you read I was a private detective who had discovered the letter, you decided to keep an eye on me. That's why you asked Mr Fisher to do some work for you. It gave you an excuse to visit him each week and buy some books in my shop. Mr Fisher found no evidence of your wife's affair because she wasn't having an affair, was she? You knew that. But you wanted Mr Fisher to follow her around anyway. The time he spent working for you was less time spent helping me with the investigation. And then you had the nerve to ask me to carry out the work when Mr Fisher stopped it!'

From the corner of her eye, she noticed Philip give her a glance. She realised she had forgotten to mention that to him.

'And then I made a mistake,' said Augusta. 'When you visited my shop the second time, Mr Ramsden, I was just about to leave to visit Louisa Bradshaw. I wanted to ask her if she had known Jemima Campbell. Just before I departed, I told my colleague that. And I think you must have overheard. You must have known Jemima was the young woman who had witnessed Alexander Miller's collapse.'

Despite all his denials, Augusta noticed a slight smile in the corners of his mouth.

'I shouldn't have said her name,' said Augusta. 'Because then she wouldn't have been threatened by you a second time.'

'You like threatening people, don't you, Mr Ramsden?' said Philip. 'Especially in the form of typewritten letters. You sent one to Mrs Bradshaw and another to Mrs Campbell. You also sent a letter to Jane Stanton pretending to be her brother. You hoped your clumsy effort would fool people into believing Alexander Miller had willingly taken himself off to start a new life.'

'As I've said, Fisher. You have no evidence.'

'I'll ask my men to seize all the typewriters in this building,' said Detective Sergeant Joyce. 'And any which are in your home too, Mr Ramsden.'

Mr Ramsden sneered. 'Typewriters? Is that all the evidence you can come up with?'

Augusta pulled an envelope out of her bag. She opened it and tipped a silver cufflink onto the table. 'Do you recognise this, Mr Ramsden?'

He shook his head but she still noticed the flicker of recognition in his expression.

'It's a cufflink which my assistant, Fred, found on the floor of my shop. It has the initials D. C. on it. Daniel Collins.'

'Those initials could stand for anything,' said Mr Ramsden.

'Fred found it on the same day you visited my shop.'

'Lots of other customers would have visited your shop that day too, Mrs Peel. This isn't evidence.'

'It's enough for now though,' said Detective Sergeant Joyce as he got up and walked over to the window. He waved to the two constables waiting outside. Then he turned back to Mr Ramsden. 'Clerkenwell police station will be happy to put you up for the time being.'

Mr Ramsden gave a laugh. 'You've got nothing on me,' he said. 'Absolutely nothing!'

Chapter 60

ROBERT STANTON WAS a diminished figure as he slumped behind his desk in his office at the bank.

Augusta, Philip and Detective Sergeant Joyce sat in a row of chairs opposite him.

'If you're here to arrest me for Jane's murder, then get it over and done with,' he said. 'But you'll be wasting your time. I didn't do it. Even though I can't provide an alibi for the time she died, I was in the Westmoreland Arms. I was there at eight o'clock. And if you're here because I assaulted that news reporter—'

'Not Walter Ferguson?' asked Augusta, with a hint of glee.

'Yes. I admit it. But he asked for it, and—'

Philip held up a hand to quieten him. 'That's enough, Mr Stanton. Perhaps you can tell us everything you know about Dr Jackson.'

Mr Stanton's jaw dropped. 'No, I...'

'If he's threatened you, then you don't need to worry anymore. He's currently in police custody.'

'Is he? How?'

'Just tell us what you know, Mr Stanton. And start at the beginning. When did you first encounter him?'

'I heard from a friend that the man behind Jackson's Blood Purifier was looking for investors. I'll admit to you now that I'm not good with money. I don't know why I've pretended to people that I am, but there you go. It's a shame, I suppose. I've made some risky investments and I've lost money through gambling. I'll admit all of it to you now. I've got nothing left to hide. Since Jane's death I've been—'

'I realise this has been a difficult time for you, Mr Stanton,' said Philip. 'But please just tell us how you first met Dr Jackson.'

'Alexander was always talking about how good Jackson's Blood Purifier was. When I heard word Dr Jackson was looking for investors for a new remedy, then I put my money in. We were promised at least double our investment back.'

'Did you meet him?'

'Yes, a few times. He seemed a thoroughly decent man. He held a meeting for his investors. There weren't many of us, so we had to put in quite a bit each. He told us all about the new remedy. Its purpose was to promote health and strength. He said he would be looking for volunteers to test it on and that he would pay well. When I mentioned this to Jane, she said she thought Alexander might be interested. He was a keen cyclist and enjoyed keeping himself healthy. And then I believe he went ahead with it and tried it out.'

'Did you ever suspect Dr Jackson could have been behind Alexander's disappearance?'

'I don't suppose I ever thought about it. Why would he have been? Oh, just a moment…' He scratched his chin. 'You don't think Alexander was poisoned, do you?'

'Yes, that's what we suspect,' said Philip.

'Good grief. So Jane was right.'

'Jane suspected it?'

'Yes. But not at the time. Only recently. It was after Dr Jackson's visit.'

'He visited you recently?'

'Yes. At our home on Baker Street.'

'And he called himself Dr Jackson?'

'Yes. It was a surprise to see him. We knew he'd gone to prison, but we had no idea what happened to him after that.'

'Why did he visit you?'

'He offered us money.'

'Why?'

'He said the business had ended so suddenly, he hadn't found the chance to properly compensate all his investors. He was very contrite and said he regretted how it had all turned out. But he had served his time and learned a lot and was now in a position to repay me with interest.'

'And you accepted his money?'

'Of course! Why wouldn't I? He was paying me back. He said we mustn't tell anyone about his visit because he'd been advised he wasn't supposed to be paying anyone back. His lawyers had advised against it, apparently. But he was doing so out of the goodness of his heart because he felt bad about what had happened. I thought the gesture was wonderful. But Jane was less convinced. She started asking him questions.'

'Such as what?'

'She asked him about the last time he had seen Alexander because we knew Alexander had been helping him test the new remedy. Then she asked if Alexander had mentioned to him if he was planning to go away. She told him she'd received a letter which was supposedly from Alexander, but she didn't believe he'd sent it.'

'How did Dr Jackson react?'

'He didn't like it. He said he didn't know who Alexander was and he made his excuses and left.'

'Why did Jane ask him those questions?'

'She thought it was odd that he turned up shortly after that news about the letter was published in the *Daily London News*. She thought there might be a connection.'

'She thought he was trying to buy your silence?'

'Yes, that's it.'

'Why didn't she tell anyone else this?'

'Because I told her it was all nonsense and that we'd been instructed not to breathe a word of his visit to anyone. We'd been given a large sum of money and I thought it was best we remained quiet on the matter. It's obvious Dr Jackson didn't like Jane asking him those questions. I think he worried that she suspected him of something. He's been arrested, has he?'

'Yes,' said Joyce. 'Do you still believe your wife's death was an accident?'

Mr Stanton rubbed his brow. 'I don't know. It sounded like an odd thing to happen, and Jane certainly wouldn't have deliberately jumped from that window. I didn't want to believe Jackson was behind it, but...'

'But you think he could have been?'

'I do now. Yes.'

'Why didn't you tell me this when I interviewed you?'

'Because I couldn't mention his visit! And I didn't want to believe it could be true. You don't know the man. There's something about him which is—'

'We've got a good measure of him,' said Augusta. 'And we have spoken with people who he has terrified into keeping silent for years.'

'Really?'

'He's a rich and powerful man,' said Philip. 'He currently calls himself Anthony Ramsden and is the director of a pharmaceutical company called Hodgson Medicines.'

Mr Stanton was speechless for a moment. 'Well I never,' he said. 'So he left prison and set himself up all over again as if nothing happened. How did he get away with it?'

'Through fear and intimidation,' said Philip. 'And he denies ever knowing you and Jane.'

'He denies it? But he was in our home a few weeks ago! And that night when Jane fell... he must have called at the flat while I was out. And she must have let him in, hoping that he might have news of her brother after all. It's been warm recently and we've kept those windows in the sitting room wide open. He must have got hold of her and...' He covered his face with his hands.

'We've got him now, Mr Stanton,' said Philip. 'And justice will be done.'

Augusta waited for him to recover himself before she asked about the assault on Walter Ferguson.

'Oh, that rat!' he said. 'He told me he'd provide me with an alibi and he didn't. I don't really know what he wanted from me, although he kept promising he would give me John Gibson's letters so we could destroy them.' He sighed. 'It sounds silly, but Jane and I wanted those letters destroyed because we were worried we'd become suspects. Jane and Alexander had fallen out over the money he lent her, and we were worried the letters contained incriminating things about us. I don't know how Ferguson got hold of the letters. Maybe he was bluffing.'

'I think he got hold of them alright,' said Augusta. 'He sent a man to my flat to steal them.'

'So he did have them?'

'A search of his home should solve that,' said Joyce, making a note.

'But why did he want them?' said Augusta.

'So he could taunt me with the idea of getting hold of them, I suppose,' said Mr Stanton. 'And I think he wanted them so you couldn't have them, Mrs Peel. He doesn't like you very much.'

She laughed. 'I'm aware of that, Mr Stanton. I shouldn't admit this in front of a police detective, but I'm quite happy to hear you assaulted him.'

Chapter 61

'DETECTIVE SERGEANT JOYCE wants us to meet him at Clerkenwell police station, Augusta,' said Philip as soon as she arrived at her shop the following morning.

'That sounds promising! But I've left Fred to manage the shop all alone for the past few days, I—'

'Go on, Augusta,' said Fred. 'I'll be fine. It sounds like you need to go.'

'Thank you, Fred.'

Augusta and Philip hailed a taxi and arrived at the police station ten minutes later. They were shown to a room where Detective Sergeant Joyce sat with Anthony Ramsden and a weary-looking grey-haired man with thick spectacles.

'Mr Havers!' said Philip. 'I haven't seen you for some time. How are you?'

'Tired.'

'Oh.'

'I've been awake all night examining letters and type-writers.'

'Thank you. Hopefully, it will have been worth your while.'

Mr Ramsden glared at them as they sat.

'Would you like to tell everyone your findings, Mr Havers?' asked Joyce.

'Of course.' He nudged his spectacles up his nose. 'I have examined six typewriters. Five of them are the property of Hodgson Medicines and one of them is the property of Mr Anthony Ramsden. I have also examined the typeface on three letters which were passed to me late last night. It's important to state that each typewriter has its own individual character. What do I mean by that? Well, these machines are designed well, but they're not perfect. To the untrained eye, a typeface from one typewriter may look very like another. But in reality, there are minor differences. Some typewriters may have one or more characters which print slightly above or below the line, while others—'

'I'm sorry to interrupt you, Mr Havers,' said Philip. 'But could we possibly just hear your conclusion?'

'My conclusion? Before I can do that, I must explain—'

'You can explain it in court, Mr Havers. But for now, please can you tell us if the three letters were typed on one or more of the typewriters you examined.'

'Were the letters typed on one of the machines? Yes, of course they were.'

Augusta breathed a sigh of relief.

'Thank you. Which one.'

'Number six.'

'And did that belong to Hodgson Medicines or Mr Ramsden?'

'It's Mr Ramsden's personal machine and is an old Remington Standard Typewriter Number Ten. It was manufactured in 1909 and is quite antiquated when compared to today's modern models. In fact, just a cursory glance at the letters was enough to make me suspect the Number Ten was used, it—'

'Thank you, Mr Havers,' said Philip. 'Your help has been invaluable. You can go and get some much-needed rest now.'

'Can I? Good. That was quick.' He turned to Joyce. 'I shall send you my full report.'

The typewriter expert left the room and Mr Ramsden sneered.

'It's a shame you don't remember Robert Stanton,' Philip said to him. 'Because he remembers you extremely well. He told us all about your recent visit.'

'He's lying.'

'Why would he lie? What would he have to gain from that?'

'This is a conspiracy against me.'

'By whom?'

'It's desperation.'

'You heard Mr Havers's evidence,' said Philip. 'You can't possibly deny you wrote those letters.'

Mr Ramsden said nothing.

'Perhaps you could finally show some decency,' said Philip. 'And explain what happened when you visited Jane Stanton on the night of her death.'

Mr Ramsden scratched his nose and glanced about the room.

'If you insist you weren't there, then you'll need an alibi,' said Philip. 'And refusing to say anything at all only makes you look guilty.'

Mr Ramsden sighed. 'She wouldn't keep quiet,' he said eventually. 'She thought I knew something about her brother.'

'She accused you, didn't she?'

'As a matter of fact, she did. Then she lashed out at me. Out of anger.'

'Really?'

'Oh yes. I had to defend myself. And we happened to be standing by an open window at the time.'

'If it was an accident, then why didn't you report it?'

Mr Ramsden laughed. 'Because you would have arrested me for murder! You would never have believed me if I'd told you it was an accident.'

'And John Gibson,' said Augusta. 'Did he lash out at you on the platform at Baker Street station?'

'That was an accident.'

'You were there at the time?' asked Philip. 'We still have all the details of the witnesses. It may have been ten years ago, but someone might recognise your face.'

'You can try, Fisher.'

Mr Ramsden's arrogant expression angered Augusta. 'You threaten and murder anyone who gets in your way, Mr Ramsden,' she said. 'You're a dangerous man who thinks only about his own ambition. Having accidentally killed Alexander Miller, you then murdered two more people who asked questions about his death. And the reason was you couldn't bear the thought of losing your reputation and your lucrative income.'

'But the irony is Mr Ramsden did lose it all for a time,' said Philip. 'The poisoning of Stephen Allen led to a prison sentence. But he was ambitious enough to reinvent himself again.'

'And ruthless enough to silence anyone who dared ask what had happened to Alexander Miller,' added Augusta.

'So no remorse then, Ramsden?' said Philip. 'No regrets?'

He said nothing.

'Not even a word on Alexander Miller's final resting place?'

Ramsden still said nothing.

'I have a theory about that,' said Joyce after the pause. He pulled a sheet of paper from his file. 'This is a map of Finchley,' he said as he placed it in the centre of the table. 'Ramsden's laboratory was here on Station Road.' He pointed to the building with his pen. 'It backed onto the railway line. As you can see, there's a bridge over the railway line which becomes Squires Lane. And just off that road, is this.' He circled his pen around a feature. 'It's a reservoir which was constructed about twenty-five years ago for Claigmar Vineyard. They grow grapes, tomatoes and cucumbers there although there's word they're going to close soon and the land's going to be sold off for housing. Anyway, it's a short walk from the building which was once Dr Jackson's laboratory to that reservoir. Perhaps the journey was undertaken in the middle of the night? With the body of Alexander Miller transported in a trolley or wheelbarrow of some sort?'

'And possibly weighed down so his remains would never resurface,' said Philip. He turned to Mr Ramsden. 'Is that what happened?'

Mr Ramsden smiled. 'They say great minds think alike, Mr Fisher.'

Chapter 62

'WE GOT HIM, AUGUSTA,' said Philip. 'And I can only hope Joyce gets a full confession from him now. I'm embarrassed I worked for Ramsden without ever suspecting him of anything. But what on earth made you suspect him? What gave you the clue?'

'It was the cufflink which Fred found,' said Augusta. 'I remember thinking about the people who'd visited the shop that day, and Mr Ramsden was on my mind. But the initials didn't match, so I dismissed the idea. Then I read about the trial of Dr Jackson and discovered his real name was Daniel Collins. I then thought of the cufflink we'd found. Fred and I had joked it belonged to David Cartwright.'

'Who's he?'

'Fred invented him.'

'Oh.'

'Those initials resonated with me as soon as I read about Daniel Collins. Then I thought again about Mr Ramsden and how he owned a pharmaceutical company. He was actually doing a similar thing to Dr Jackson, only with more credibility. I also knew the person behind Alexander Miller's disappearance was keeping a keen eye on our investigation. Louisa Bradshaw and Jemima Campbell were threatened. Jane Stanton was murdered. The culprit had to be close by.

'And then I realised Mr Ramsden had only appeared on the scene after the newspaper report about the long-lost letter had been published. It seemed a fantastical thought, but I couldn't put it out of my mind. What if Mr Ramsden was watching us? And when I realised Mr Ramsden and Dr Jackson were the same age and had come from the same place... I was determined then to find some evidence to support my theory.'

Augusta thanked Fred when they got back to the bookshop. 'I couldn't have done it without your help,' she added.

'Oh, I didn't do much.'

'Yes, you did. We did it together,' said Augusta. 'All three of us.'

'Yes, I suppose we did,' said Philip. 'And with a bit of luck, Walter Ferguson will be charged after sending someone to steal those letters from your flat.'

'That was Walter Ferguson?' said Fred.

'Apparently so,' said Philip. 'And the unpleasant man he paid to do that will be tracked down and charged with assaulting Augusta.'

'I'd almost forgotten about that,' said Augusta.

'How can you have forgotten? You broke a rib!'

'I'm just relieved we got Ramsden and that Ferguson's article was never printed.'

'Two very good reasons to be relieved,' said Philip. 'I think we need a drink to celebrate.'

'Good idea,' said Augusta. 'I'll put the kettle on.'

'Kettle?'

'What's wrong with that?'

'I was thinking of something stronger.'

'At eleven in the morning?'

'Well, it's not every day you solve an obscure case which has evaded everyone for ten years.'

A short while later, they stood at the counter with a cup of tea each. Augusta sipped her tea and felt a warm gratitude towards her colleagues. They had become more than colleagues. They felt like proper friends now.

'I'm happy Ferguson's article was never published,' she said. 'But I feel like I owe you both an explanation.'

'An explanation?' said Philip. 'No Augusta. You don't owe us anything.'

'There's something I want to tell you. I trust you both and I don't want you thinking I'm hiding anything from you.'

'We don't think that,' said Fred.

'Even so. It's time I told you the truth.'

Chapter 63

'I CHANGED my name when I joined British intelligence during the war,' said Augusta.

'We all did,' said Philip.

'Yes. You called yourself George Whitaker. But you went back to being Philip Fisher again, didn't you? I kept the name Augusta Peel because... I feel like Augusta Peel. That's who I am.'

'You don't have to explain yourself, Augusta,' said Philip. 'We know you as Augusta Peel and that's all there is to it.'

'But I want to tell you now. Having prepared myself for my secret being out in the open, I realise now that I'm ready to talk about it.'

'Alright then.'

She took another sip of tea. 'There are a few reasons why I don't use my real name,' she said. 'I suppose the main reason is that I'm estranged from my family.'

'I'm sorry to hear it, Augusta,' said Philip.

'I've led a very different life to the one they wanted for

me. They wanted me to become a wife and mother. But I wanted to do lots of other things first.'

'That's understandable,' said Fred.

'I had everything I needed as a child. I received a good education. I had a governess, then went to school.'

Philip raised an eyebrow. 'A governess? Was your family wealthy? Oh, sorry. You don't have to answer that.'

'The governess bored me,' said Augusta. 'She had wiry grey hair and an enormous nose. She taught me and my sisters and I'm afraid my behaviour was quite poor. My governess told my parents they should send me away to school.'

'Boarding school?'

'Yes. In Berkshire. And I actually really enjoyed it. Unlike many other girls, I was delighted to be away from home.'

'And how old were you at this time?'

'Ten. I had some good teachers, and I did well there. I learned a lot. And so it seemed strange to me when I turned sixteen that all my parents could talk about was finding me a husband. I was resistant to the idea. As punishment, they sent me to boarding school in Switzerland for two years. My parents clearly hoped the place would refine my manners and attitude. I perfected my languages while I was there and I found opportunities to get out and explore the area. Sometimes I had the school's permission and sometimes I didn't. But I enjoyed it. It was better than being at home.

'I was eighteen when I returned home and my parents introduced me to the man they wished me to marry. While I had been away, all the arrangements had been put in place.'

'They didn't ask your permission?' said Philip.

'No. They were convinced they knew what was best for

me. The date for the wedding had been arranged and all the guests had been invited.'

'No!' said Philip. 'That really is quite astonishing! I realise things were a little old-fashioned when we were young, Augusta. But to actually choose your husband for you and arrange your wedding without consulting you at all? That really is beyond belief.'

'I was very unhappy about it. His name was Bartholomew, and he had a very long surname and a receding chin.'

'Even worse.'

'I had some terrible arguments with my parents about it. Nothing would change their minds. So there was only one way out. I left them and came to London. There was a family friend in London and she helped me. She disapproved of the way my parents had treated me. So I stayed with her and her husband for a short while until I could find a job and pay rent for myself. I found a job in a library.'

'So you've always loved books, Augusta.'

'Yes, I have. As soon as I could read, books provided me with a sense of escape. I read all the time when I was away at school and working in a library was the perfect environment for me. But I realised I could earn a little more money with some more skills. So I went to secretarial college and learned shorthand and typing. After that, I worked for a theatre company.'

'Theatre?'

'Yes. I typed scripts and helped organise things behind the scenes. And that was how I met Matthew Peel.'

She hadn't said his name aloud in a long time.

'He was an actor,' she continued. 'Not well-known at all. He was the same age as me and had been doing it for about ten years. He hadn't had a lot of success and I'm not sure he was very good at it, really. But we fell in love and we planned to get married. It was 1914 and, for the first time in my life, I felt truly happy. I was estranged from my family and I felt enormously sad about that. But I had met Matthew, and he understood me and made me laugh. I met his family and got on well with them all. I finally felt like I belonged somewhere. We had a lot of fun together and our relationship seemed like the most natural thing in the world. And then he went away to fight.'

Silence followed. Augusta knew the next part of her story needed little explanation. 'He had only been gone two months when I received a letter from his family. He was killed in action at the Battle of Loos.'

'Oh, Augusta. I'm so sorry,' said Philip.

'When he died, I felt the need to do something different. I saw a mysterious advert in the *Evening News* asking for well-educated, independent women. I was intrigued and didn't know what I was applying for. I had to sit some tests and, after that, I met our mutual friend Mr Wetherell in the cafe on Tottenham Court Road.

'When I realised I was working for British intelligence, I was determined to do my job well. I didn't want Matthew's death to have been in vain. So that's what motivated me. Although I look back now and realise that the whole reason for the war made little sense. Matthew was one of millions who lost their lives. Everyone knew at least one person who didn't come home. And in that respect, I don't consider myself much different to anyone else.'

'But you didn't have your family for comfort at a time like that,' said Philip.

'No. But I found comfort in other things. And after the war, my comfort became books again. That's how I found myself repairing books in a basement.'

Philip smiled. 'Who can forget your basement workshop, Augusta. It was very dark and dingy down there. You really have made progress since then. And I understand now why you chose the name Augusta Peel. Matthew would have been your husband if the war hadn't happened.'

'Yes, he would have been.' Augusta tried to ignore the lump in her throat. 'But events were beyond our control. There really wasn't anything different we could have done.'

'One question,' said Philip. 'Who was the family friend in London who helped you?'

'Oh, that was Lady Hereford.'

'So that's how you know her!' said Fred.

'And I'm afraid I have to ask another question,' said Philip. 'Your family could afford a governess and sent you away to school. Lady Hereford was a family friend. Who exactly were your family, Augusta?'

Augusta paused. It felt awkward to say it now, she didn't feel a part of them anymore. 'The Buchanan family.'

'The Buchanans? I've not heard of them. But that's because I don't move in the right circles. Are they landed gentry?'

'I suppose so,' said Augusta. 'My father has a title.'

'A title? I'm guessing it's not Mister.'

'No. He's the Earl of Uppingham.'

Philip's mouth dropped open. 'An Earl?'

'I've had nothing to do with him for nearly twenty years.'

'He's an Earl?' Fred's eyes were as wide as saucers. 'So what does that make you, Augusta? A lady?'

'If I were to use the name I was born with, then I would be called Lady Rebecca Buchanan.'

Chapter 64

THE SHOP DOOR swung open and Lady Hereford entered, pushed in her bath chair by her nurse. Fred dashed over to hold the door open for them.

'Good morning!' said Lady Hereford. 'Goodness, what have I missed? You could cut the atmosphere in here with a knife.'

Augusta nervously cleared her throat. 'I've just told Philip and Fred my real name.'

'They didn't already know it?'

'No.'

'Oh. I thought you would have told them by now.' She grinned at them. 'Surprising, isn't it?'

'You were clearly very supportive of Augusta when she had no one else,' said Philip.

'One just does what any normal person would do.' She addressed her nurse. 'Wheel me over to Sparky, please.'

Augusta knew Philip's compliment had embarrassed Lady Hereford. She didn't know how best to respond to praise.

'I've become so accustomed to calling her Augusta that

it's strange to think she's really Rebecca,' said Lady Hereford as she fed Sparky some birdseed. 'I knew the Earl of Uppingham and his wife for many years, and they had three delightful daughters. Two were happy to marry into good families and have done well for themselves. The other one, however, had a mind of her own.' She gave Augusta a broad smile. 'And she was always my favourite of the three.'

Now it was Augusta's turn to feel embarrassed.

'The earl and his wife made a mistake when they tried to arrange a marriage for Rebecca,' the old lady continued. 'I warned them she wouldn't stand for it, but they didn't listen. And so they lost her. It's a terrible shame because they're missing out on a great deal.'

Augusta felt the lump in her throat again. 'You've been like an aunt to me, Lady Hereford.'

'Well, that's nice to hear, Augusta. And I think that makes Sparky your cousin.'

Augusta laughed.

'Having heard your story, I think you're very brave Augusta,' said Philip. 'Other young women in your position would have gone along with their parents' wishes.'

'They would have done,' said Lady Hereford. 'They wouldn't have wanted to lose their money and privilege.'

'My freedom was always the most important thing to me,' said Augusta. 'Being a lady meant little to me. I don't mean any disrespect, Lady Hereford, because I know it means a lot to some people. It's a shame my parents had such rigid expectations of me.'

'It's their loss, Augusta,' said Lady Hereford. 'They've missed out on seeing what their wonderful daughter is capable of doing.'

Augusta rarely gave her parents much thought these days. It pained her to think about relationships which were over. The estrangement from her parents had left a gap in her life which would never be filled. Occasionally, she wondered if they ever thought of her. She knew they couldn't possibly be proud of her, because she hadn't done what they had wanted her to do.

'I sometimes wonder if they ever regret it,' said Lady Hereford.

'I hope they regret it,' said Philip. 'I don't understand it! We live in an age now where most people are receiving a good education and women can work as well as men. To restrict people's dreams and ambitions seems very old-fashioned to me.'

'It is old-fashioned,' said Augusta. 'And it was twenty years ago. It was a different time then. Everything before the war feels like a different time.'

Everyone nodded. 'It does,' said Lady Hereford.

'Once the war was over, I felt determined to make a new life for myself,' said Augusta. 'I didn't want to dwell on what had happened in the past.'

'That's understandable Augusta,' said Lady Hereford. 'But that doesn't mean forgetting about the people who are no longer with us.'

She was talking about Matthew Peel. Lady Hereford had adored him.

Augusta nodded and felt tears at the back of her eyes. 'No. We can do more to remember them.'

She only had a few photographs of Matthew and they were hidden away in a drawer. She had last looked at them after Philip had picked them up from the floor of her flat after the break-in. She made a promise to herself to talk more about Matthew from now on.

He needed to be properly remembered.

The End

Historical Note

Baker Street is famous for being home to a fictional address for a fictional detective. Sir Arthur Conan Doyle published his first Sherlock Holmes story in 1887, and the detective featured in four novels and 56 short stories until 1927.

Baker Street was named after William Baker who built its rows of smart Georgian terraces in the 18th century. These days, the street is just over half a mile long and runs from Regent's Park to Portman Square, just north of Oxford Street.

Madame Tussaud opened her famous waxworks on the street in 1835 before moving to nearby Marylebone Road. Famous past residents include the 'father of science fiction' H.G. Wells, the novelist Arnold Bennett, Prime Minister William Pitt The Younger and singer Dusty Springfield.

But what about Sherlock Holmes? He lived at 221b Baker Street - an address which never existed.

In the first half of the 20th century, parts of Baker Street were rebuilt. Down came many of the Georgian terraces and - after some renumbering too - the imposing

Art Deco headquarters of the Abbey National building society occupied 219–229 Baker Street. Abbey National received so much mail addressed to Sherlock Holmes that a secretary was employed to reply and explain the fictional detective had retired to West Sussex.

In 1990, the Sherlock Holmes Museum opened at 237-241 Baker Street. An argument ensued between the building society and the museum about who should receive Sherlock Holmes's mail. The responsibility eventually fell to the museum after Abbey National vacated their head-quarters in 2002/05 (reports vary on the date). The museum has obtained permission from Westminster City Council to use the address 221b Baker Street. Even though it's fictional!

Sherlock Holmes superfans have attempted to locate where 221b would have stood, based on descriptions in the stories. There's a theory that the building Conan Doyle chose was at the southern end of Baker Street on the west side. As this part of the street has been extensively rebuilt since Conan Doyle's day, we'll never know for sure.

There's nothing too remarkable about Baker Street these days. It's a mixture of shops and offices with the little museum at the top end. Some of the original Georgian terraces remain, but much of the street has been redeveloped (the area suffered bomb damage in WWII).

Opening in 1863, Baker Street station was the first underground railway station in the world. Today, it comprises three different underground stations and is served by five tube lines. As a major interchange and popular tourist location, it's a busy place.

The 'accidental' death of John Gibson was inspired by a tragedy which happened to my grandfather's cousin exactly one hundred years ago. He was nineteen years old and had been on his way to work when he fell in front of a train from the busy platform of West Ealing station. What struck me about the inquest reports was how much the witnesses disagreed with each other. Some said the fall was accidental, while others said it was deliberate. The coroner eventually decided on a verdict of 'death by misadventure'. There was never any suggestion of foul play, but I wondered just as Augusta did: if the platform was so busy, how could anyone be sure? In my family's case, I'm certain it was a tragic accident.

Jackson's Blood Purifier was inspired by 'Clarke's World Famed Blood Mixture'. It was a popular tonic in the late 19th and early 20th centuries and claimed to cure most ailments, including rheumatism, sores, scurvy and gout. When the British Medical Association examined the product in 1909, it was found to contain water and sugar with a little bit of alcohol, ammonia and chloroform. It was medically quite useless. The medicine wasn't unusual for its time, but the British Medical Association was concerned by the proliferation of these 'secret remedies' and published a book in 1909 called *Secret Remedies - What They Contain*. The book revealed the contents of these medicines and accused their creators of behaving unethically. A person named in the book was Major Charles Henry Stevens who had created 'Umckaloabo' while in South Africa to cure tuberculosis. The remedy sold well in Britain and he tried - unsuccessfully - to pursue a libel case against the British Medical Association. Modern examination of his remedy has revealed it may have contained some health benefits.

In the 1891 Sherlock Holmes story, *A Case of Identity*, Holmes proves that a letter has been written on a specific typewriter. Conan Doyle was ahead of his time because this story was written three years before the handwriting expert, William E Hagan, stated each typewriter produced its own peculiar type. The first part of the twentieth century saw a number of court cases where typewritten documents were forensically examined for evidence.

Finchley is a suburb of north London these days, but its history can be traced back to the 13th century. The area was predominantly farmed until the arrival of the Great Northern Railway in the 1860s. Speculative Victorian housing developments followed, and the area was swallowed up by London's rapid growth between the wars. These days, it's a popular residential area. Finchley was the constituency of Britain's first female prime minister, Margaret Thatcher. She represented the area as a Member of Parliament from 1959 to 1992.

Death in Kensington

An Augusta Peel Mystery Book 8

Killer couture: murder is in fashion

A high-society fashion show is not Augusta Peel's usual idea of entertainment. But when she's offered a spare ticket, the chance to see a show by a renowned designer is too good to miss.

The glittering event takes a turn when a rising model is found dead after the show. Augusta embarks on a murder investigation where the glamour of fashion collides with the deadly secrets of the wealthy. And as the stakes are raised, Augusta must use all her wits to unravel the threads before someone else becomes a victim.

Find out more here: mybook.to/death-kensington

Thank you

Thank you for reading this Augusta Peel mystery, I really hope you enjoyed it!

Would you like to know when I release new books? Here are some ways to stay updated:

- Like my Facebook page: facebook.com/ emilyorganwriter
- Follow me on Goodreads: goodreads.com/emily_organ
- Follow me on BookBub: bookbub.com/au- thors/emily-organ
- View my other books here: emilyorgan.com

And if you have a moment, I would be very grateful if you would leave a quick review online. Honest reviews of my books help other readers discover them too!

Also by Emily Organ

Penny Green Series:

Limelight
The Rookery
The Maid's Secret
The Inventor
Curse of the Poppy
The Bermondsey Poisoner
An Unwelcome Guest
Death at the Workhouse
The Gang of St Bride's
Murder in Ratcliffe
The Egyptian Mystery
The Camden Spiritualist

Churchill & Pemberley Series:

Tragedy at Piddleton Hotel
Murder in Cold Mud
Puzzle in Poppleford Wood

Trouble in the Churchyard
Wheels of Peril
The Poisoned Peer
Fiasco at the Jam Factory
Disaster at the Christmas Dinner
Christmas Calamity at the Vicarage (novella)

Writing as Martha Bond

Lottie Sprigg Travels Mystery Series:

Murder in Venice
Murder in Paris
Murder in Cairo
Murder in Monaco
Murder in Vienna

Lottie Sprigg Country House Mystery Series:

Murder in the Library
Murder in the Grotto
Murder in the Maze
Murder in the Bay

Made in the USA
Columbia, SC
05 May 2024

35312244R00159